A young man's quest to lift a
terrible curse upon his people

Forest
nymphs

The Joining of the Shadows

GERARDO SURZIN

A young man's quest to lift a
terrible curse upon his people

Forest nymphs

The Joining of the Shadows

GERARDO SURZIN

MEREO
Cirencester

Mereo Books

1A The Wool Market Dyer Street Cirencester Gloucestershire GL7 2PR
An imprint of Memoirs Publishing www.mereobooks.com

FOREST NYMPHS: 978-1-86151-852-1

First published in Great Britain in 2017
by Mereo Books, an imprint of Memoirs Publishing

The address for Memoirs Publishing Group Limited can be found at
www.memoirspublishing.com

The Memoirs Publishing Group Ltd Reg. No. 7834348

The Memoirs Publishing Group supports both The Forest Stewardship Council® (FSC®) and the PEFC® leading international forest-certification organisations. Our books carrying both the FSC label and the PEFC® and are printed on FSC®-certified paper. FSC® is the only forest-certification scheme supported by the leading environmental organisations including Greenpeace. Our paper procurement policy can be found at www.memoirspublishing.com/environment

Typeset in 12/18pt Century Schoolbook
by Wiltshire Associates Publisher Services Ltd. Printed and bound in Great Britain by Printondemand-Worldwide, Peterborough PE2 6XD

About the author

Gerardo Surzin was born on 25 November 1981 in Slovakia. Over the last ten years he has lived in many different countries, included Australia, Singapore and London, thanks to his work as a Lead Environmental Artist, Art Director and Concept artist for feature films working on projects such as *Hunger Games, Pacific Rim, Clash of the Titans* and many more. This work has also give him an opportunity to do oil painting, with several exhibitions around Asia and Europe. He has always wanted to write a fantasy novel to express his love for the fantasy worlds that could exist. The title "Forest Nymphs" made the perfect connection with nature.

Filmography info and portfolio:
www.surzin.com
http://www.imdb.com/name/nm3123878/

Special thanks

There are a number of people I would like to thank for their help with this book. First may I say a special thank you to my family for their support. Thank you Maria, Jan, Roman, Milos and Jovi!

Special thanks also to my friend Creative Director Samat Algozhin, who was very closely involved into the story structure and its development. Thanks Sam!

samat.algozhin@gmail.com

Also to my friend Co Art Director Waldemar Bartkowiak, who was involved in developing the details of the characters. Thank you Waldek!

mancubus3d@gmail.com

Then to a writer, Jean Esther, who was involved in developing the story line with me. Thank you Jean!

naej83@gmail.com

Special thanks also to traditional artist Morena for her support. Thank you Morena!

Finally my thanks to Chris Newton, my editor at Mereo Books, for his editing and guidance over various details of the manuscript. Thank you Chris.

Contents

CHAPTER 1

A Darkening Sky

Aragel flopped onto his back with a weary sigh, eager to take a break from working in the fields. He could hear his friend Erien calling out to him from behind the haystacks, but he was too lazy to reply. Instead he kicked off his boots and watched his friend's scruffy black hair bob along above the haystacks as he searched for him.

"Aragel, where are you?" Erien yelled for the fifth time. Aragel closed his eyes and wondered how his mother was back at home. She had sprained her back, leaving him to work in the fields alone.

"Time sure crawls when you work alone," he sighed to himself.

"Aragel? Is that you back there?" Erien called out again.

"Damn it... Yeah, I'm here."

"Why didn't you say anything when I called the first time? Were you even listening to anything I was saying back there before you disappeared?" Erien was a little annoyed that Aragel would disappear on him like that.

"Well... not really," Aragel replied, smiling cheekily. Erien's eyes narrowed at the sight of his friend lying on the haystack, and Aragel sat up, feeling slightly guilty. They were supposed to have been working in the fields to provide for their families.

As far as Aragel could remember, Erien had always been in his life. Standing seven feet tall, he towered over just about everyone. But there was something about the friendly grin that often spread across his tanned, rugged face that made people feel comfortable around him, making him an easy person to confide in. Though they never talked about it, Aragel worked hard to provide for his mother and Erien would help out wherever he could. His mother had had a hard life raising Aragel alone after his father had passed away a few years ago. Remembering all this made Aragel feel even more guilty for shirking his duties. He really should be more responsible.

"So, I reckon you heard?" Erien suddenly asked, changing the subject. He was grinning like a young schoolboy, breaking Aragel out of his reverie. Aragel looked blankly at him.

"Um, no? What are you talking about?"

Erien snorted in disbelief. "You know, about Virto and his plans to…" A loud rumble of thunder muffled his words. Curious, Aragel tilted his head to see the sky. Thunderstorms were rare in Morenia. The light azure sky had darkened with low-hanging clouds, a sure sign of impending rainfall. It had not rained in weeks and the downpour would prove to be wonderful news for the farmers and their crops, but something felt different about the wind this time. Something that pulsed in the air sent shivers down Aragel's spine, making the hair on his neck stand on end. He'd never felt this way before, but he knew that something was wrong. He remembered when his father had told him tales of impending bad luck when the wind blew the wrong way, and he was starting to think that this might be one of those times.

"What are you getting all anxious about? It's just a storm," Erien reasoned. "Maybe it looks scary because it's been a long time since we've had one." He was trying to make sense of the pang of fear that had shot through him. He could feel something too, but he was always the logical thinker, and he wanted to present an answer that would satisfy that part of him that didn't believe in omens and magic and bad luck.

Aragel looked out over the high point of the hill where they stood and felt his nerves loosen a little as he gazed out over his village and the slanted shadows of trees along the hills. Arya was a beautiful village surrounded by towering hills with rolling green pastures and sharp hidden rocks embedded in the angles of the hillsides. Aragel remembered when he was younger how he and his friends used to dare each other to climb the sharp rocks, just to see who would do it. Many a time had one or more of them fallen, and his friends had to carry him home to his mother to bandage him up.

Aragel smiled slightly at the sight of his beautiful home, but just then something caught his eye that made the hairs on his neck stand up again. People were running in all directions, several pulling their children away from the fields and dragging them towards the houses. Sickles, harvesting baskets and other farming paraphernalia were left behind as men, women and children fled from the fields. They looked as if they were shouting, but their voices, garbled by the wind, became unintelligible sounds. Nothing would make them run away from the fields to seek shelter in their homes, certainly not a thunderstorm. In this village, you worked until the job was done, and if you happened to get rained on, well so be it.

"What the hell is going on down there?" Aragel muttered. "Something is not right. It's as though these people are trying to escape from something." It truly looked as if the poor village inhabitants were trying to outrun one of the mythological monsters that Aragel had read about. His father used to read the stories of all the heroes and gods to him, and of course they included monsters. Now it seemed as if maybe one of his stories had come to life.

"Or maybe they're just trying to warn the others about the storm?" Erien was deep in thought. Aragel could tell that he was trying to come up with a logical explanation. If there wasn't a logical explanation for something, then Erien just couldn't be at peace with himself.

"Yeah, maybe, but why do they need to leave their tools behind? No one living in Arya or the neighbouring villages would run from a storm like that," said Aragel. Erien knew Aragel was right, but his timid nature would not allow him to think about what could be lying over the horizon. He wasn't as imaginative as Aragel, and he definitely didn't spend any of his time reading mythology, so even if he'd wanted to, he couldn't dream up a monster as Aragel could.

On the far left of the hillside that stretched out before them, a limping figure was waving a stick at everyone running past him, but no one took any notice. Aragel smiled in spite of himself. Most villagers tried to stay out of Roley's way, but to Aragel, he had become the father figure he needed after the death of his own father. With eyes that twinkled and the smile of a young man behind a full beard, Roley was the wisest, kindest man Aragel had ever met, even if he enjoyed poking his nose into other people's business every now and then, sometimes even starting rumours just to see how people would react. The village as a whole considered him to be a drunk just because he liked his alcohol, and they thought he was crazy because he would tell stories of the old days when fairies and other creatures were there to help the humans that had moved into their home.

To Aragel, he was a kindly soul, but to the villagers, Roley was a grumpy old man who was rude, intrusive and hateful. Eccentric in his own way, Roley was not one to listen to what others had to say, often having fixed opinions about things and people. Over time, rumours began to spread about who Roley really was. Some people believed he was jealous because he had had his youth stolen by an evil wizard years ago. But those that didn't believe in magic, or refused to think that anything like that could happen in their little village, believed he had been ill-treated as a child by his parents, and therefore sought joy in making the lives of others miserable. With rumours like that in a village with about 1500 people, it was not difficult to understand why half the population hated him. But to a group of three inquisitive young men, he was a grandfather, a tough, unyielding but kind soul who has always been there to guide them, making them understand what it meant to be responsible people.

"Ah, the old man, in the middle of all the action as usual," Erien grunted in wry amusement. "What's he up to now?"

Aragel peered across Erien's shoulder. He could not make out what words Roley was screaming, but he waved when their godfather looked in their direction. "I don't know, maybe he's yelling for us to get home before it starts to rain."

Cupping his hand against his mouth, Aragel yelled as loud as he could manage, "We know, Roley! We'll head back soon!" He waved again, smiling at him to show him they understood. The old man's reply was lost in the howling wind.

Erien shot Aragel a questioning look and Aragel shrugged. It was probably nothing. He lay back down and stretched out against the hay again, relishing the cool, crisp air.

The haystack rustled and shifted a little as Erien

plopped down beside him. "Good day to sleep in, huh?" said Erien, yawning. Aragel couldn't agree more. It was the perfect weather to snuggle under the covers and be as unproductive as possible. Even though that was what he liked to do, he wished sometimes that he had a pretty girl to snuggle under the covers with. Otherwise, what was the point? Other than sleeping, anyway.

"Yeah, but that'll never happen. Even if I was snuggled under the covers, Ma would drag me out and make me clean the house." Aragel sighed heavily in resignation as he thought how his mother would never let him do what he wanted. He never got to anyway, no matter what the weather was like.

A strong gust of wind beat against Aragel's face. He winced, pushing aside the dark brown hair that flopped over his eyes. He wondered if Ma would cut his hair. It was getting longer and was beginning to curl out in all directions, sitting on his shoulders in a haphazard mess. Or maybe he should just keep it growing until it reached his waist. He imagined being able to bring his hair forward and braiding it, smiling a little at the thought. Then he might be mistaken for a girl, but it would be a good joke anyway.

"What's so funny?" Erien asked, seeing Aragel's goofy smile.

"Nothing, just a silly thought," Aragel said, turning

his attention to Erien and imagining with a smile what his friend would look like if he had long plaited hair.

Suddenly a bright flash lit up the sky, pulling Aragel out of his reverie. Erien and Aragel exchanged nervous glances and looked up. Lightning was never a good sign. Five summers before, Aragel had had to provide a temporary home for their neighbours when a stray lightning bolt had struck their fields, burning their entire crop. Months of hard work and dedication had burned to ashes in a matter of hours. He remembered his mother pulling him aside, whispering how lucky they were that their fields were untouched by the lightning, and declaring that Aragel must always protect their fields. 'Those fields are all we have left from your Pa,' he heard her say, as she buried her face in her hands that day. That had settled in Aragel's heart, and he'd done whatever was necessary to protect the fields from that day on. But how could he protect them from lightning?

"Run, you stupid fools!" Roley bellowed, closer now. Startled, Aragel lost his balance on the haystack and fell, cursing while Erien sniggered at his ungracious form on the ground. When had Roley got here? How had the old man managed to get up this slippery slope so quickly with a cane? Not to mention the sharp rocks that jutted out at intervals along the way. He must have flown up here.

"It's coming here!" Roley jabbed the stick at them and looked pointedly at the sky. The sky gave another ominous rumble as they looked at it, as if to emphasize his point.

"What's coming?" Aragel said, feeling a bruise blooming on his buttocks. If anyone saw that, he would never hear the end of it.

"What's coming, Roley?" Aragel repeated as he grabbed Erien's outstretched arm and stood up. Roley looked visibly disturbed, his grey hair falling in a tangled mess, framing his pale, gaunt face. His eyes darted wildly as if in search of something. He was shivering and his hands gripped the stick tightly as his lips moved in fervent prayer. Something terrible had to be coming to frighten the old man like this. He was tough as nails, and there was nothing that could scare him, or at least, so Aragel thought. He looked nothing like the calm and unassuming Roley they knew. Even the usual mischievous twinkle in his eyes was gone. Something was terrifying him, and he was trying to protect them from whatever it was.

There was a heartbeat of silence before Roley's mumbled prayers stopped. Aragel thought that maybe whatever it was that had scared him was gone, but the next second, Roley indicated otherwise.

"It's here! Can't ya feel it?!" Roley suddenly shrieked, letting out a loud haunting wail that frightened Aragel and Erien. It reminded Aragel of the banshees that he'd read about, except that they were women and they only shrieked like that when someone was about to die. Roley, on the other hand, had never made such a sound in his life, as far as Aragel knew. This must really be bad.

Aragel hesitated for a second before shaking his head. There was no point in trying to understand Roley when he was this distraught. Roley was now hunched over himself, eyes wide with an understanding that was lost on the two younger men. For a brief moment, Aragel thought that it might be better not to know what was going through Roley's head right now. He knew he had to do something before he strained himself and got hurt.

"We've got to calm him down," he whispered to Erien. "There's no way he's going to make it down safely going on like that."

From where they stood, it was a long way down for Roley's brittle, ageing bones and he had no idea if Roley would actually leap off. Given the state of mind the old man was in, anything could happen, and Aragel was not about to take any chances. He'd already lost one father, and now that Roley had become the new father figure he'd needed, he wasn't about to lose him too.

"You sure he'll calm down?" Erien said, looking

increasingly uncomfortable with each passing whimper from the old man. He wasn't exactly good at things like this. He was a thinker, and he used his brain to work out difficult puzzles, but when it came to human emotions, he was lost. He would rather turn and run the other way, because emotions weren't logical, and he didn't know how to handle them.

"I don't know, but it's worth a shot," Aragel muttered, taking a step towards Roley. It was like approaching a baby deer, each step careful and calculated. Roley was still walking around aimlessly, staring up at the sky, but he wasn't praying any more. Had he accepted whatever he was afraid of? Or did he know that there was nothing that could be done and feel he might as well stand there and take it?

"Roley, it's Aragel," he said softly, "Calm down. Take a deep breath, and tell me – exactly *what* is coming?"

Dull, frightened eyes looked back at him. It seemed he was about to say something, but then Roley just crossed his arms defensively across his chest. He wasn't acting like an adult any more, he was acting like a frightened child. Aragel knew better than most that it was sometimes impossible to reach a frightened child with just words. Confused and tired, he decided to stop trying. He might just push the old man over the edge if he kept pressing. At this point, what mattered the most was keeping him safe and out of danger. Erien's strong presence was reassuring; it would have been a real challenge bringing Roley down on his own.

"That! The sky!" Roley broke his silence with a whisper. He was still staring up at it, and now he was trembling. Something was really scaring him, and there was nothing that Aragel could think of to do to save him from his fear except to get him home as quickly and as carefully as possible.

"The storm?" Erien asked gently. He was trying his best to reason with Roley. If he could just figure out what the old man was afraid of, then he would know how to rationalize it and help him.

"No! No! No! Why don't you see it?" Roley seemed almost desperate now, as if he couldn't believe that they couldn't see what he was trying to show them.

"Because you're not making any sense, Roley!" Erien retorted, losing his patience.

Fixing a stare on Erien, Roley scrambled close to him, jabbing the stick skywards. "The sky Erien... look at the sky!" Erien did as he was told and looked upwards.

"It's just a storm, Roley. Nothing bad will..."

"It is not a storm!" Roley snarled before Erien could finish, swinging around suddenly to grab Aragel's shirt. Aragel steadied himself by grasping Roley's shoulders and smelled the acidic retch of alcohol and vomit on Roley's tattered shirt. Well that made more sense now. He had been drinking again, Aragel realised, taking a step back in case Roley threw up on him. Whatever was in the sky was only visible to Roley, and the two of them still couldn't understand what had the man so distressed. He must have been hallucinating from drinking so much. That was the only explanation that Aragel could come up with.

"It's coming here!" Roley exclaimed, bursting into sobs and loosening his grip on Aragel's shirt. Erien grabbed Roley from the back and held him up as Aragel watched. He was thankful for Erien's brute strength; he could hold Roley up with one arm.

"C'mon, let's go before he loses it again," Erien said, laying Roley down on the haystacks. "He'll sober up on his own and he'll be back to himself in no time."

Aragel was inclined to agree with him, but for some reason, he just didn't know if this was an alcohol-induced hallucination or something that he just couldn't see. The stories and myths came back to him, and his brain was on overload trying to think of something that might coincide with the sky during storms.

"Hang on," Roley mumbled, trailing off. Aragel stopped, much to Erien's frustration. *We can't leave him like that*, Aragel mouthed. With a big sigh, the kind-hearted giant relaxed his shoulders and rubbed his temples. Aragel smiled. Beneath his tough exterior, Erien's heart was gold. That was why the two of them were friends. Aragel tended to wear his heart on his sleeve, while Erien hid his feelings until they were needed.

Satisfied that his audience was not going anywhere, Roley settled in against the haystack with a sigh. Aragel and Erien both wanted to groan in frustration. How were they supposed to get him home if he curled up in the damn haystack?

"It's not a storm," Roley started. He seemed more sober now. "It's something else – all the rage, all the hatred in the air. Can't you feel it?"

Roley looked at Aragel and Erien, his eyes begging them to understand what he was trying to say. "I'm speaking the truth. Run or it'll be too late! The rage and hatred... they..." he stopped. "It does things. Unspeakable things."

Aragel thought he might be on the path to believing that something really was in the sky, now that Roley had explained what they should be looking for.

"If this thing you speak of is unspeakable, then why are you speaking to us about it?" Erien mocked. He was trying to make light of the situation, and Aragel didn't blame him. It was easier to shrug or laugh off the warning than to believe that there was something malevolent in the sky.

"Stop it Erien, can't you see he's trying to tell us something important?" said Aragel. But Roley had already clammed up. Lips tightened in a scowl, he began to hobble away. He was outraged that no one wanted to believe him. He had come up here because he thought these two would be the ones to listen to him and take heed of his warning.

"You kids think you know everything, you will regret not believing me. I'm telling you the truth!" Roley insisted, striking his stick on the ground. He started to take his frustration out on the soft and yielding ground, punishing it as he stabbed his stick in the earth over and over again.

With a sense of unease, Aragel watched Roley hobble away. At least he was safe. The old man's drunken ramblings sounded crazy. Still, the desperation swimming in his eyes had been genuine. Roley was afraid. A retired top-notch hunter who had dealt with wild animals on a daily basis was actually frightened… but of what? It hardly seemed possible he would be afraid of a storm. This was the first time he had seen Roley lose control of himself and it spooked him. It was the first time he had seen Erien behave so arrogantly as well. Maybe there was some truth to what the old man was trying to say. All Aragel knew was that nothing felt right.

CHAPTER 2

Behind the Painting

"It's not like Roley to lie or to behave that way," Aragel said, turning to see Erien looking uneasily at the darkened sky. "Think it's real?"

Droplets of rain started pelting their cheeks. The two friends groaned in unison. They had been so caught up in Roley's ramblings that they had forgotten to set up the temporary nets. Whenever there was rain, the farmers would prepare large netted cloths that spanned their fields to prevent the crops from drowning. The nets were held up by sturdy poles that stood over each square plot. Excess rainwater would be collected in self-dug channels along the fields that distributed water as evenly as possible. It was a tedious but cheap way of watering the crops. It was crude, but it worked.

They raced down the hill, workboots squelching against wet grass. Rain poured steadily from the skies, then grew to a torrent as they reached the foot of the hill. The wide expanse of greenery could no longer be seen; a grey veil of rain shrouded their vision. Only a local could navigate through the heavy rain without guide.

Aragel dashed towards the muddy fields, shouting for Erien to grab the netted cloth as he drove the poles deep into the soil. He worked quickly, eager to get out of the pouring rain.

"Shit, damn it!" he cursed as his hand slipped, giving him a splinter. The long wooden poles were hard to drive in, and everyone would always wear gloves for the job, but since they'd been lollygagging in the haystacks and were now in a hurry, there was no time to go back for the gloves, so he would just have to suffer the consequences. He made a mental note to keep his gloves on his belt from now on. He was distracted.

Roley hadn't answered his question about what was arriving in Arya, and it was still bothering him. "What the hell were you trying to say, Roley?" he murmured. He was talking to himself, or maybe the pole, he wasn't quite sure. He rammed another pole into the soft soil, this time making sure he was careful not to get splintered again. There was a tingly sense of déjà vu he could not quite shake off. There was something going on, something greater than he could comprehend, and It was beginning to frustrate him. He liked to have a plan for any occasion, and not knowing what was coming made that a little difficult. He cursed again as he got another splinter for thinking instead of watching what he was doing.

Finally back inside his rustic, orange-roofed, stone-walled cottage, Aragel fell into a rickety armchair and stared at the bright yellow walls of his cosy home. Yellow and orange were his father's favourite colours and it was at times like this when he felt lost that he missed his father the most. He looked out the window and imagined his father walking down the pathway in his scruffy worn-out brown coat and work boots. Had it really been two years already? He put his head in his hands. The rain had stopped as quickly as it had started. If it had not been for the glossy sheen of leaves and the damp ground, no one would have been able to tell that it had rained at all.

"Aragel, are you going to take a shower or are you going to sit there in that chair all evening?" came Aragel's mother's voice. To the villagers she was known as Mrs Brise, but to those closer to her she was just known as Brise. At sixty, Brise looked like she was still in her forties. With her perfect pale complexion and dark auburn hair, no one would have guessed she had a grown son.

"Yes, Ma, I'm going to take a shower right now," he answered. He trudged upstairs to the bathroom and turned on the hot water. When the steam began to rise, he climbed in, trying to wash the uneasiness away with the rest of the day. As he let the hot spray hit his back, he couldn't help but think back to Roley's words. It was true that he'd felt something, but he hadn't been able to see whatever it was that Roley had tried to warn him about. The hot water turned his skin pink, but he didn't care. He liked feeling like he could wash the worries and problems of the day away with a steaming hot shower.

Now if only he knew what Roley had been trying to warn everyone about. It was obvious that he'd been shouting at the villagers to warn them, but he still didn't know what he'd said, so he wasn't quite sure what to make of the situation.

It was at times like this that he really wished his father was here. He would know exactly what was going on, and what to do to prepare for it.

He got out of the shower and dried himself off, heading to his room to change. Finally in some dry clothes, he picked up the steaming mug of cocoa his mother so reliably prepared for him every evening and sipped at it as his Ma prattled on about the odd weather. She had fussed over their shivering bodies when they stumbled in from the rain, and got to cooking large bowls of soup to warm them after their baths. Erien had made his way back home a few minutes before; he had been forced into Aragel's father's old clothes and looked extremely uncomfortable in a shirt that was too close-fitting for his liking and pants so short that they flapped around above his ankles.

He could hear his ma fussing about in the kitchen. The cottage was a cosy space for two people. A curtain separated the living den from the narrow kitchen; there were stairs just outside the kitchen, and a room beside it that was used for storage, since it was too small to be a guestroom. On the second floor, three rooms lined up next to each other along a corridor.

The dreary atmosphere was killing Aragel's appetite and he was beginning to get restless. Finishing the rest of his cocoa, he started pacing before the fireplace, stopping every now and then to throw in more wood. The fire crackled, spitting red embers every time Aragel prodded it or threw in more.

Bethany! He suddenly remembered. He was supposed to make some toys out of wood for Bethany, a little girl who lived two fields away. Seeing that he had nothing else to do, Aragel took his carving knife to continue chipping away at the palm-sized wooden pieces. It was a relaxing hobby, one he indulged in whenever he wasn't working in the fields, spending time with his best friends Erien and Virto, or helping his Ma with household chores. Maybe focusing on the little pieces of wood would put his mind at ease more than the shower had, because right now he didn't feel like it had done anything to get rid of his worries.

He glanced out of the window again. A deep frown crossed his face; the dark clouds showed no sign of fading away. Oddly, they looked closer than before, and the villagers were busy packing their possessions and throwing makeshift covers over their gardens and crops. It felt like the entire village was waiting for something to happen. Even his neighbours had bolted their doors for protection. But protection from what?

He could understand their anxiety – the clouds had now turned into a menacing inky blackness which was quite unnatural. There was nothing to prove that they were unnatural; it was just a feeling that he had. What Roley had said suddenly felt a lot more ominous. It suddenly felt like there really was emotion in the clouds, and they were going to rain down their anger and hatred on the little village of Arya. But why? And since when did clouds have emotions?

He shook his head. Trying to understand

everything was only going to make his head hurt. He wished Roley had explained. "It's not a storm. It's something else – all the rage and hatred!" What did that even mean? He sighed and tried to block it all out of his mind so he could work on the wooden toys.

Roley was sure that the clouds were the key to whatever was going on. It felt strangely familiar... he knew he had heard something like it before, but where? And from whom? Aragel mumbled to himself as he dug the carving knife a little too roughly into the toy figure. His thoughts began to drift back to a simpler time, and Aragel began to reminisce...

"What's in that bag, papa?" a young, ten-summers-old Aragel wanted to know.

"Secrets, my child, one day you will know." There was a mischievous twinkle in his father's eye as he answered him without really answering him.

"Why can't you tell me? You're always keeping secrets," Aragel whined as his father pulled him in for a hug.

"The bag carries stories, Aragel my son. Of heroes and monsters, of sadness, hatred and rage, but most of all, stories of bravery, kindness and love," his father whispered in his ear.

"Will you tell me these stories?"

"Sure."

Aragel smiled. His memories made it feel like his

father was closer to him.

"Aragel! Dinner!" yelled his mother breaking him out of his daydream.

"The bag, Pa's bag, I have to find it, there might be something in there," Aragel muttered to himself, ignoring his mother completely. Feeling the beginning of an adrenaline rush, Aragel dropped the toy and accidentally brushed all the wood shavings onto the floor as he pushed back his chair too hard causing it to fall with a loud thud. The noise drew his Ma from the kitchen.

"Aragel, you aren't a child any more. Stop making more work for your mother!" She nagged as she bent to sweep the mess, wincing from the pain her injured back caused her. Aragel smiled sheepishly, giving his ma a one-armed hug before taking the broom and dustpan from her to clean the mess he had created. His mind was churning through everything that his father had ever told him about that bag, but none of it gave him a hint as to what the contents could be.

"Sorry Ma, I got up too fast." He felt a little guilty about making her clean up after him, and he knew that she did her best to hide the pain that she was in. Even though she always said that it wasn't too bad, he knew she was lying, because he could hear her softly crying into her pillow some nights.

"You young people never know your strength, but

I promise you will when you get old like me. Now, why don't you tell your ma what's wrong? And don't even thinking about lying," she added, "I'll know if you do."

That was a mother's gift. No matter what, she could always tell when he wasn't telling the truth, or when he was upset about something, or when he was doing something that he shouldn't be. Sometimes he wished that she would just get caught up in something, maybe village gossip, and let him get away with something every once in a while. It was difficult to lie to the woman who had raised him. Still, he couldn't possibly tell her what Roley had said. She would just freak out. Besides, he wanted to search his father's belongings, and there was no telling what his mother would say if she knew he was going to do that. Especially if she found out that it was only based on Roley's crazy paranoia.

"Ma, I just remembered that Pa had this... bag," he gestured uncertainly. "It's big and wide, so I thought it could be put to use instead of lying around." He was hoping that she wouldn't ask him what exactly he wanted to use it for, because he really had no idea what he could say. He just needed that bag, and right now, he was willing to do whatever it took to get it. He wanted to solve this mystery. It was something that he knew his father would have done, and he wanted to be like him.

"You and your Pa, peas in a pod. Always finding some way to use something twice." She shoved him towards the stairs, gently. "I think it's upstairs, in his workroom. He never put anything in order. Wouldn't be surprised if it takes you more than a day to find it under all that junk. Now shoo, I have a table to set for dinner."

He'd got lucky. Not only had she narrowed down his search, she hadn't even asked him any questions. The adrenaline was pumping through him now, making him feel like he was invincible. He was going to get that bag.

"Yes Ma'am!" Aragel bowed with a dramatic flourish to mask the excitement he felt. Ma used to have a wet shine in her eyes whenever they talked about Pa, but nowadays they could laugh and joke like close friends, sharing memories of the man who had supported their world with broad, strong shoulders. Now it was Aragel's turn to do the same, and he would honour his father by loving his mother twice as much. It was now his responsibility to watch over her and make sure that she was taken care of, and in his own humble opinion, he was doing a pretty good job of it.

The floorboards creaked as he went up the stairs and straight to the end of the narrow corridor. He had not stepped into his father's workroom for a long time. It had been a sanctuary when his father had been alive, and somehow it had just felt wrong to go in there alone. It used to be a room that filled him with wondrous awe whenever he was inside. His Pa did not forbid him from touching his things, so he was free to look through his father's scribbles even when he had not learned how to read. There had been fascinating trinkets, their shapes and colours now a hazy blur in Aragel's mind. He could remember long days spent in there, by his father's side, as he crafted one thing or another. It never got boring, no matter how many times his father tried to get him to go out and play instead of sitting on the floor, craning his neck up to see what was going on.

He stood in front of the wooden door, fingers curled around the brass doorknob. Inhaling deeply, he twisted and pushed. The door swung open noiselessly, revealing a patterned cloth spread across different parts of the room. He could make out the shape of a table under one of them. Crossing the threshold, he did not know what to think. Was he expecting something different? It looked nothing like the room of his memories. It felt like a graveyard. When he had been here with his father, every little piece of wood or metal had life to it, and had seemed to his childish mind to glow with energy. Now it looked like a dead room, where no life had ever been. It broke a piece of his heart, but he knew that the memories would always be there for him when he needed them. After he found the bag, he wouldn't have to come in here again.

Aragel started pulling off the patterned sheets of cloth, noting that that each one carried a different design. He coughed at the tiny dust clouds that had risen, and then looked around the room once again. It seemed like only yesterday when he had been able to climb into the huge wardrobe that sat in the corner of his father's room. It was probably the best place to start looking. After all, the room was a mess.

His father had been a hoarder and the wardrobe was filled with trinkets and treasures, so it was difficult not to get distracted. Aragel found a dagger with an elaborate letter A intricately carved into its handle, a copper bottle with red precious stones set in a uniquely-shaped star and a stone-like pendant threaded through an old piece of leather string. Putting his head through the necklace that he assumed was his father's, he reminded himself what he was there for and started his search for the bag again. He had to find it today; he was willing to skip dinner for it if he had to.

The room was a treasure trove of memories, a place where he had spent his childhood exploring imaginative lands with his father. Sitting on the mantelpiece was a little toy soldier he remembered his father making for him. "I made this soldier to protect you, son," he remembered his father telling him. He tried to tell himself that the moisture in his eyes was only from the dust. Taking the toy soldier off the mantelpiece with a shaking hand, he put it in his pocket. How could it protect him if it was here on the mantelpiece?

He opened the drawers of the dark hardwood cabinet next to the mantelpiece, looking through each one and finding nothing. The last drawer would only pull out halfway. "Ugh, it's stuck," he grunted. He didn't know if he was complaining to himself or to the soldier in his pocket, but the drawer was definitely stuck, and he was struggling with it.

A musty smell that came from it made Aragel take a step back. He frowned. Well, he was already here, he might as well overturn every drawer. But the foul, musty smell filled his nostrils. "Ugh," he coughed, looking into the drawer. He had found the source of the smell – a dark brown, frayed leather sack-like bag with a rusty clasp. "Yes!" he exclaimed quietly. He had found the bag.

He quickly unfastened the clasp to find pieces of worn, yellowing parchment inside, and saw that there was writing on them. He pulled them eagerly out of the bag, tearing the edges of a couple of pages in the process, unable to contain his excitement as he started reading.

"Once upon a time, in the far reaches of the world, there was a benevolent man..." he read softly, immersing himself in the familiar words. It was one of the first stories his father had read to him as a child. It was about a caring man who had rescued an injured fairy, who had then thanked him by promising to grant him one wish. The fairy knew that the man's wife and child had just passed away, so she offered to use the wish to bring them back to life. To her surprise, the man turned her down and told her that he just wanted a friend. So the fairy stayed to become his friend. Years later, on his deathbed, the fairy stood by his side and the kind man held her hands and thanked her for being such a good companion all this time, 'It is my turn to go on a long journey now. My wife and child are waiting,' he said. The fairy, now alone and overwhelmed with grief at the loss of her friend, cried for a long time until finally she became a willow tree that stood over the graves of the man and his family.

"Do you know what the story is about?" Aragel's father had asked as he had tucked little Aragel into bed that night.

"Is it about fairies and the wishes they give you?"

His father shook his head sadly. "No son, it's more than that. This story reminds us that no living being can live without somebody else to share their joy and sadness with. You understand?"

Aragel nodded, but he did not understand; at least not until Pa had passed away, leaving him with the realisation that it was just him and his mother now, and all they had to rely on was each other.

He placed the parchment on the floor and skimmed through the rest for any sign of the words 'rage' or 'hatred'. There were still several pieces inside the sack-like bag. Holding the drawer's handle with one hand and its side with another, Aragel yanked back harshly, losing his balance as he released the drawer and bumping into something that dug against his hip. He yelped as it struck the bruise he'd got earlier from falling off the haystack and hitting the harsh ground.

He paused for a moment, then listened hard to make sure that his mother hadn't heard him and was now on her way to investigate what exactly was going on up there. He didn't hear anything, so he breathed a sigh of relief. He grabbed it without thinking, righted himself, then glanced at what he had knocked into. It was a beautiful painting of the sun setting in Arya, but it had been knocked from its position, revealing a pale imprint left by years of hanging at the same spot.

There was something strange about the painting. He touched it and the faded bronze frame felt heavy in his hands as he shifted it to the side to take a better look. The picture had pressed into the wall, leaving a rectangular imprint against the otherwise even wall.

Curious, Aragel knocked on it with his fist, and the hollow sound told him that there was a cavity behind it; it was a false wall.

Why hadn't Aragel known about this? Maybe his father had intended to share his secrets with him when he got older, but had never got the chance. He stared at it, confused by what he had found. When had his father done this this? And why? What was he hiding? Questions streamed through Aragel's mind. He knew that he would have to find a way into the wall to0 get some answers.

His mother's voice floated up from downstairs. "Aragel, you better come down for dinner or I'll never cook for you again!" He smiled. It was an idle threat, one she had used very often, too. When he'd been younger he had thought she meant this threat, but now he knew better.

He stared at the impression in the wall, wishing he could work on it right away. But it would do him no good to upset his Ma. Uncovering the mystery of the hidden compartment would just have to wait till she was asleep. With one last lingering look, Aragel pushed the painting back into place and made his way downstairs.

CHAPTER 3

The Mystery Deepens

Later that night, after checking that his mother was sound asleep, Aragel re-entered his father's workroom with a bag of tools. First he examined the area around the painting. He soon figured out that there was no mechanism, hidden or otherwise, to open the wall.

He removed the painting carefully and placed it on the floor, then wrapped several rags round a hammer to muffle the noise he was going to make. Taking a deep breath, he smashed the wrapped hammer against the dent. He stopped, listening for any sound of movement from his mother's room, which was just two doors away. Only a quiet chorus of crickets answered. Reassured that she hadn't heard him, Aragel swung the hammer again. Cracks appeared. He had been right! He had to stifle a whoop of triumph.

He stopped, listened, then continued, repeating the cycle again and again and watching the cracks deepen. It was a good thing his mother was a deep sleeper. He wondered if his father had kept the secret from her as well.

Aragel pushed against the widening cracks and pried the stubborn covering away bit by bit until the hole was big enough to admit his arm. It was now clear that there was a large open space behind the wall. He peered into the darkness, trying his best to make out what lay behind the wall. "Should've eaten more carrots as a child" he mumbled to himself, breaking off more chunks of the wall and smiling. His father had always told him that carrots were good for his eyes. Aragel had asked him how he knew, and he'd simply said, 'I've never seen a rabbit with glasses, have you?' When he was a baby, his mother had even made up a little song about that to make him eat his carrots.

Finally he managed to create a hole big enough to squeeze through. He blinked a few times, trying to adjust his eyes to the darkness, and stepped inside.

"Ow!" He had walked right into an old brown chest of drawers. He peered down at it, and saw that the chest was engraved with intricate markings along its sides in a strange pattern of never-ending curves. He ran his fingers along them. Then he tugged against the heavy lock and it gave way easily. Pa never did like using locks anyway, he thought with a smile.

He dragged the chest out onto the floor of the room, where he knelt to take a closer look at its contents. It was full of books and papers. Aragel stared at the neat rows in surprise. He did not remember his father being a tidy worker. It was usual to see his belongings thrown haphazardly as he wrote furiously onto scraps of parchment. Whatever these documents were, they must have been important to be kept so neatly.

Aragel took one of the books and began to flip through it. There were many pages. One section was about how deer should be trapped, with instructions for how to skin them. He frowned, flipping through the following pages until he reached the end. There was nothing to throw any light on what Roley had been ranting about.

He brought the lamp closer and picked out another book, then sat on the hard floor with a heavy sigh as he started reading. It was going to be a long night.

***

Clean shaven with chiselled features, Virto, the

youngest of the group of friends at twenty-three, was also the brainiest. He prided himself on being a calm person, considering that he could keep up with his best friend's crude impatience and tendencies to go on rambling for hours. He was a humble man, never forgetting his roots. Even as a learned scholar, he never turned his nose up at spending a day out in the fields helping Aragel and Erien with their crops. But even his tolerance had a limit.

"What's your problem, Aragel? It's way too early for a mystery," he grumbled. He had been dragged out of bed before dawn and was still dressed in his night clothes, which offered very little protection against the morning chill. He had been hauled to Erien's tiny house, where he was thrown to the ground and treated to a torrent of words that made little sense to his sleep-addled mind. Aragel had added to Erien's rant every now and then, waving pieces of paper that fluttered meaninglessly in front of Virto.

"Let me get this straight," began Virto. "The two of you dragged me here in the middle of the night – no, Erien, I don't care that it's going to be dawn soon. You two saw fit to bring me here just to tell me that the dark clouds that have been there since a week ago are not normal?" His voice was dripping with sarcasm, and if his eyes hadn't still been gummed half-shut with sleep, he would have probably taken a swing at one or both of them.

"Hang on – a week?" said Aragel, frowning. "These clouds appeared out of nowhere only yesterday."

"No they didn't," said Virto coolly. "I've noticed them moving towards the village for a while now. I figured they were just a prelude to a thunderstorm, that's all. So I don't get why you two are getting your tights in a twist over them." He was still lying on the floor, and if these two would just shut up, he could get back to sleep... even if it wasn't on his feather bed.

"Those clouds are bad news!" insisted Aragel.

"Roley was sayin' something about rage and hatred and then Aragel here shows up with this..." interjected Erien.

"And I can't understand what's going on if the both of you keep speaking at the same time," Virto said, rubbing his eyes. "All right. Let me freshen up, give me something to change into, and then tell me everything. Slowly."

He was hoping that by the time he freshened up and came back, the two of them would be gone. He intended to take a long time. His friends were eager to comply; Aragel pushed him towards the washing area at the back of house, while Erien rummaged through his wardrobe in search of some decent clothes for him. In a bid to calm himself down, Virto started reading the documents. Reading always did something to him to make him calm his mind and relax. It was something he'd discovered when he was a child. He had been teased at school for being smart, and had come home and told his mother about it. She had smiled at him gently, and handed him a book. He could still remember her telling him that it was better to use his angry energy to learn something. That was why he had wanted to be a scholar.

Finally Virto, dressed in Erien's spare clothes, rejoined his friends, who were looking uncharacteristically solemn. He listened to Erien's account of what happened the previous day, from finding Aragel resting in the middle of his work to Old Man Roley's drunken ramblings, and eventually being roused from his sleep by an excited Aragel carrying a large brown chest. When he had made sure that he had registered every detail of Erien's story, he turned to Aragel and asked him to recount what had happened.

"I must have spent two hours going through everything in Pa's chest," Aragel said, his deep-set eyes betraying a hint of worry. "It was weird but I couldn't keep Roley's words out of my head. They were somehow familiar. Father had told me something like that before but I still can't remember most of it. I found this though." He picked up a thinly-bound book and handed it to Virto, who opened it carefully. He began to read aloud.

"I have travelled widely and seen many breathtaking places and people," he read. The most beautiful thing I have ever witnessed was in the Forest of Axter, and those graceful bodies dancing in a circle as they laughed and sang. It made me feel a happiness I had never before experienced, not even when my child was born. Even the dark clouds could not resist their power... I know now that they are the key to warding off the rage and hatred..."

Virto read through the rest of the book in relative silence, then asked for something to write on. Erien handed him some pieces of parchment, a half-filled ink pot and a barely used quill, and then Aragel and Erien left him alone and went off to prepare breakfast.

Virto's mind struggled to make sense of what he was reading. He knew that Aragel was dying to know what he made of the other documents in the chest, and frankly, Virto was just as curious, though he hid it well. There was no use in getting his friends any more excited than they were already.

"What did you think of it?" Aragel's voice snapped him out of his thoughts. It's a little difficult to compose your thoughts when there's a face in your face.

"Get out of my face, man!" Virto pushed his friend away as Erien settled on a chair a size too small for him. "From its contents, I have determined that this chest contains the works of your grandfather's travels." Virto proudly held up what he had scribbled, glancing at Aragel. "And while most of them talk about his hunting trips and there's a fascinating discussion on methods of killing the animals, there are some entries that mention what Old Man Roley had said to the both of you. 'Rage' and 'hatred' are the key words and, based on…"

"Tell us something we don't know." Erien rolled his eyes impatiently, remembering Roley's cryptic rant.

"…what was written," Virto continued sharply. He didn't like being interrupted, and when it came to an achievement or a speech that he was making, it was twice as rude, in his opinion. "Those two words were mentioned when Aragel's grandfather talked about what he had seen during his travels," he went on.

"In the Forest of Axter, right?" Aragel interrupted. "And some… unknown beings or something like that?"

"Yes. The mysterious unnamed beings who made your grandfather feel… incredibly light and peaceful were apparently the key to 'warding off the rage and hatred' and that 'even the dark clouds could not resist their power'. Now I'm not sure if those dark clouds are the same ones your grandfather was talking about, Aragel, but they might be, considering Roley's strange behaviour and the stuff he was going on about."

"So we need to find this out. We need to find these unknown beings or creatures. Maybe they know something about all this."

Virto shook his head. "And what are you planning to do? Play the superhero and run off to find the Forest of Axter on your own without even knowing where it is?" Virto knew Aragel's impulsive streak all too well. Aragel flinched at Virto's condescending sarcasm. "That is what a fool would do, Aragel. These were written a long time ago. We don't have any proof that something bad will happen. Does the Forest of Axter even exist? How long will it take for you to find it? And if those dark clouds are really harbingers of doom, what will happen to our village while we're out there?"

"I..." Aragel started, then faltered.

"I don't like the look of those odd clouds either, Aragel, but I'm not going to plunge into something without getting my bearings right."

"Gotta agree with Virto on that one, Aragel," Erien finally chimed in. Aragel was not happy at having his friends outvote him two to one, but what could he do to persuade them, otherwise?

"But we have to do something!" Aragel argued, pushing his chair back as he stood. "Who knows what might happen if we don't? You weren't there, Virto! You didn't see the look in Roley's eyes, he was scared out of his mind." The image of the old man trembling and shaking, his eyes dulled with fear, was something he wouldn't be able to get out of his mind, probably for the rest of his life. No one deserved to be that terrified of something. If he could find a way to save Roley ever having that look on his face again, he would. He couldn't just sit back and do nothing.

"I never said we would just sit back," Virto said, packing the books back into the chest. "I just mean we need to get more information first. Even the smallest bit would do." Aragel was slightly mollified, but it still wasn't a guarantee that yes, they were going to do something.

"And where would we get it?" Aragel asked, putting his face in his hands again out of frustration.

"As you said, I wasn't there. And since the two of you have no clue what's going on, the most logical choice would be asking Roley, yes?" Virto said, trying hard not to sound as if he was scolding Aragel. He stood up unhurriedly. "Now let's get going."

***

Finding Roley was not hard. The old man was slumped outside his door, eyes wide and unseeing, damp with perspiration and beer. His faint rancid smell made Virto stop some distance away. Aragel rushed towards him, and worry filled his eyes as he spoke to the dazed man in a soft, concerned tone.

"Roley? Roley? Can you hear me?" He started to slap his cheeks to try to wake him up.

"Is he...?" Virto said nervously, hanging back as Erien went forward to join Aragel. Being around dead bodies was one of his biggest fears, but so far he'd been able to hide that fact from his friends. If Roley was dead, and he was standing this close to a dead body, it wasn't just his friends who would find out but the whole village. He could already feel a blood-curdling scream working its way up his throat.

"No, he's not dead," Erien said, snapping his fingers in front of Roley's blank gaze. "But I don't know why he isn't responding to us."

Aragel frowned. Was Roley in a catatonic state? Had something happened to him yesterday after the young men went home? What was going on?

"Should we get Thelia to look at him? She'd know if he's ill," Aragel said uneasily. Thelia was the village medicine woman, and she knew how to cure every single ailment the village had ever come across. She was a little older than Aragel and his friends, but she was still as beautiful now as she had probably been ten or twenty years ago, and her face was ageless.

Virto watched with forced calmness. Something was wrong; he had been standing in Roley's line of vision, yet the old man was looking right through him as if he wasn't there. Like he was nothing.

He frowned, turning to see what Roley could be looking at. "The clouds," he said. "He's staring at the clouds." Aragel and Erien turned to follow his gaze, then looked back at Old Man Roley's face.

"That's it," Erien growled, shaking Roley's shoulders. "I've had enough of this. Roley! You know something, don't ya?"

"Stop shaking him!" Aragel pushed Erien. "That's no way to treat Roley."

"E-enough," a hoarse voice rasped brokenly. Roley pulled away from Aragel's steady hold on him. "Go away. I have nothing to say to you. Any of you."

Roley started to try to pull himself to his feet, but it wasn't going his way. Finally, he just gave up and collapsed back to where he'd been sitting, staring at the clouds.

Virto gritted his teeth. How could he say that? Though he had never been very close to him, Roley had always been kind to them, especially towards Aragel after his father's death. Erien too looked up to the old man as a mentor and advisor, someone he could turn to whenever he got into ugly spats with his own father. Virto knew his relationship with Roley wasn't as close compared to Aragel or Erien, but he had never had any reason to dislike the older, wiser man. Right now, however, Virto was tempted to knock some sense into Roley.

"All right," Aragel said softly, "I'll come by later."

The trio of friends made as if to leave. Breaking out

of his violent thoughts, Virto suddenly realised how angry he really was. His face had grown hot and his fists were tightly clenched. Erien approached him hesitantly, looking between Aragel and Roley. Virto looked away. He could hear Aragel coaxing the old man to go into his house. Then he heard shuffling footsteps as the older man complied, and the quiet click of a closing door.

"Now what?" Erien said tiredly. The look on Aragel's face was just as weary, and he glanced back at Roley's house as if he wanted to stay.

"He'll be fine, Aragel. Besides, it's not the end of the world," Virto said. "Just because Roley isn't talking it doesn't mean we've hit a dead end. In fact, there's someone in the village who has an eye and ear out for everything that goes on."

His friends turned to him with blank but eager faces. Now it was his turn to be the font of wisdom. He puffed his chest out a little, relishing the moment.

"Who?" Aragel and Erien said at the same time.

Virto smirked smugly. "Who's the biggest gossip in our village?"

CHAPTER 4

A Warning, and a Plan

An old, unused chandelier hung over empty crooked rows of square tables. Matching benches, chairs and stools had been left in different positions, some knocked over, as if their previous occupants had pushed them back carelessly. Candles had sunk into themselves, offering what little flame they had left to light the place.

In the semi-darkness of the Winged Maiden, wrinkled hands were wiping empty mugs. Igedian, now reaching his seventy-fourth year, was in a bad mood. Business was slowing for the only bar in Arya.

There was hardly anybody coming in any more and with the recent unpredictable weather, most villagers preferred to stay indoors, in the comfort of their own homes. Having served only ten customers so far that night, Igedian decided that it would be wise to close for the day and get some well-deserved rest.

"Hey, wake up." He nudged Bronson the farmer, his only remaining customer. Bronson's Bloodshot eyes met Igedian's, then closed again in favour of resting on the table. But Igedian was not about to get dismissed in his own establishment, and he shook the man roughly. "Go home if ya wanna sleep," he said. He thumped Bronson's back and laughed heartily when he groaned in protest. It'd be so much easier if his little girl was there, he thought, she was much better at getting these lazy bums back home than he was. She was much nicer about it, too.

That thought made him smile. It wasn't exactly that he took pride in being mean and cruel, it just came naturally to him, and he'd never bothered to rein it in very much. His smile faded at the thought of his daughter, all dazzling smiles and bright-eyed wonder. They hadn't spoken in years. No use thinking about her now. She'd made her choice and he'd made his.

"A'right, time to go, Bronson ol' boy," Igedian said gruffly. "This ain't a bedroom." He prodded the man's back with an almost empty mug, scowling when the farmer barely budged. "Suit yerself. Gonna be putting this on ya tab again," he grumbled. Sometimes, if the patrons didn't want to go home, Igedian would let them spend the night, but he would charge them the same amount as if they had rented a room to sleep in. It was a good way to get customers home at the end of the night.

The wooden door rattled to the sound of polite knocking. Bronson mumbled in his sleep, head lolling sideways. Igedian ignored the knocking in favour of counting the bottles of beer. No one ever wanted to talk to him, and he had already decided that he was going to close early. No one was going to make him change his mind. "Eleven... twelve... er, thirteen." When the knocking got louder, he rolled his eyes and shouted, "We're closed!"

The door burst open to reveal three outlines standing at the entrance, the morning sun shielding their faces. Igedian felt the shelf underneath the bar for his rifle in case these people were looking for trouble.

"Wait! It's me, Virto!" Igedian squinted and, sure enough, as the figures stepped forward, he recognised the trio. Erien's hulking figure dwarfed his companions as he stepped across the threshold into the Winged Maiden. Igedian remembered that he was a blacksmith and known for his strength. At this, he lowered the rifle and levelled a glare at the other two. Virto, a scholar – the only one in Arya, even if he had no idea how and where the young man had got his supposed qualifications – had the courtesy to look away. He was the second youngest of the group and probably the brightest.

Igedian's gaze reached the last of the trio – Aragel. So much like his grandfather, Igedian thought. Even his eyes looked like those of the stubborn old git.

"Whaddaya want? We're closin' for the day," he said, then waved at Virto to shut the door behind them. Though Igedian was not in the mood for idle chit-chat, the looks exchanged between the trio made his skin itch. He had a hunch this was a conversation that he wouldn't be escaping from, at least not easily. And something told him this wouldn't be a conversation that he wanted to have, much less one he would want to be overheard.

"We're sorry for disturbing your rest, but…" began Virto.

"Tell us about the Forest of Axter." Aragel's demand cut across Virto's curt apology.

Igedian stiffened. "I dunno what you're saying," he said brusquely. "Sorry, can't help ya."

"You must know something," Virto said confidently, unrolling a parchment as he stepped towards Igedian. The young man's eyes were shining with excitement.

"Aragel's grandfather wrote of this forest and while I cannot bring myself to believe in something unless I've actually seen it, we have a number of documents that seem to prove it is real."

Hardly aware that his face had paled, the old publican looked away. Yes, he remembered when Aragel's grandfather had come into the inn, talking about all the wonders and beauty of his travels...but he also remembered a few of the dark things that he'd discovered, and Igedian had always been an eager listener. He'd thought that it wouldn't hurt to indulge him, especially since none of it was true. Then the old man had started to bring proof...

"So it does exist!" Aragel, perched on the edge of his seat, looked pleadingly at Igedian. "Surely you know something? Something odd is going on. Roley was ranting about rage and hatred. I found these things by my grandfather, and it all comes back to one thing – the dark clouds."

"Not to forget the mysterious beings that Aragel's grandfather saw in the forest. Whatever they were, they could get rid of the clouds," Virto interjected angrily, standing up with fists clenched. His analysis was never wrong. Erien pushed him back into the seat.

Igedian shook his head stubbornly. It would take more than that to drag the dark secrets out of him.

"I dunno what's got into you all. This conversation

is over!" he snapped.

"But the stories! I can't remember much, but my father had told me things about the Forest of Axter when I was still a child," Aragel said. He was very persistent, and he didn't want to give up on this. There had to be an answer to all of this and an explanation for the clouds rolling over Arya.

"You go there then, if you wanna die!" Igedian's yell rang out in the silence. He took deep, gulping breaths of air and got off the chair, making his way to his usual spot behind the bar counter. He refused to look at the trio, unable to hide how anxious he felt at the thought of Aragel going anywhere near the dreaded forest. These were good boys, and he didn't want them to risk their lives for nothing. He'd heard quite a few stories about the forest, and they all talked of at least one man lost searching in it, or for it.

"It's too damn dangerous. No one knows what happened to those who ventured inside, and those who tried to find a way out never came back." He took a piece of rag and rubbed it against the table with unnecessary force. He got nervous when the talk turned to things he didn't want to think about, so he was trying to keep himself busy and focus on something else. "I don't know much. Went to the Forest of Axter myself, many years ago, but..." Igedian paused. "Then I turned back. I didn't see anything."

His voice dropped. "Talk to Adomah. She might have more to say."

Igedian heard Erien thanking him as he attempted to drag his friends out of the bar. He bustled around, pretending to be busy, then waited till the door shut before he collapsed onto the chair. He closed his eyes, suddenly overcome with regret. Seventy-four years was too long; he wanted to be young and innocent of the world again.

***

"He's hiding something," Virto declared as soon as Erien had pulled them – not without some protest from Aragel and Virto – out of the Winged Maiden. He wanted to pry for more information from Igedian. The innkeeper had looked as if he was going to say something, but then changed his mind at the last second. It was nearly impossible to get Arya's infamous gossiper to stop talking once he started and, in Virto's eyes, such uncharacteristic behaviour was telling.

"What I don't get is why you were being so unreasonable," Aragel said. "Shouting at Igedian is not very helpful. Your scribbling wasn't much use either. Igedian could barely read it."

"Anything's better than hitting an old man," Erien

quipped quietly. Virto stared at his friends.

"I didn't hit him."

"Because I stopped you," Erien said.

"I wasn't going to hit Igedian!" Any argument between the friends could turn into a powder keg, so it was usually a good idea to stop it before it got started.

"Hey, hey, let's not start fighting each other," Aragel's soothing voice washed over them, clearing Virto's head of all the harsh words he had been about to say. A glimpse at Erien showed that the other man was feeling the same way. He reluctantly offered an apologetic nod. Usually, that job fell to Aragel, so he was used to it by now.

"Guess we must have not slept enough," Virto said tersely, his gaze not quite meeting the others' eyes. When no responses came, he continued trudging forward. "Let's go find Adomah."

The walk to Adomah's cottage was surprisingly uneventful. There were some curious glances from villagers, prompting friendly waves from Erien. Aragel did not understand why Virto was being so quiet, but he did not pursue the matter, knowing that they might end up arguing again.

At that thought, his chest thudded painfully. Why was this happening? He disliked seeing his friends argue with each other. Virto had sacrificed his time to rearrange and write down whatever they had found in his father's chest, while Erien had stayed by him through the unpredictable turn of events so far. When this was over, he would get the two stubborn fellows to apologize to each other. Each of them had had an integral part of this mystery, and so it was only fair that they all get along in order to figure out what the clouds meant.

"We're here," the scholar said, coming to a stop before a cottage. Virto was panting, a slight sheen to his forehead that made his hair stick to his skin. It was then that Aragel realised they had reached the top of the highest hill in Arya.

Despite the tension between his friends, Aragel could not help admiring the view. He could see the swaying wheat fields, light golden and stretching across several acres, intersected by with rectangular patches of fields of different colours. Beyond them he could see the dark expanse of the Great Wood far in the distance, and grey mountains looming up behind them and disappearing into the sky. The clouds were still there, black and uncomfortably close to the village.

He turned to see Adomah's house and its small garden lined with red bricks, filled with vivid colours that were uncommon in the village. The cottage itself was plain, cream and brown with streaks of vine tendrils running up along its walls. Everybody in Arya knew about Adomah, the stark raving mad woman who lived alone, isolated by the rest of the village. It was believed that looking into her eyes would bring bad luck. Whether it was for that reason alone, or for reasons that the friends did not know, everyone avoided her whenever she came down from the hill. Some villagers would go as far as to burn their clothes after being near the woman, thinking that it would cleanse them of her infectious madness. Even Aragel's mother had warned him of the woman, saying that she was not right in the head and that it was better to stay away from someone like that. "Witch!" the children would whisper amongst themselves, yet wanting badly to prove that they were not frightened by her.

Once, as a child, Aragel had dared Erien and Virto to thrown stones and pebbles at Adomah's window. They had run away once they'd heard the door creaking open, afraid that the mad woman would throw them into a boiling pot. And here they were, standing outside the home of their childhood's superstitious fear, because Igedian had said she knew something. Somehow, there was a poetic justice to that, and Aragel was still in a position to enjoy the irony. Looking at his friends' faces, however, he didn't dare bring it up right now.

Aragel's knuckles rapped against the door.

"Adomah, please open the door! We have something important to ask you."

There was the sound of bolts being lifted before the door clicked open, creating an inch-wide gap that allowed the trio to peer in curiously. A cobalt blue hood prevented Erien and Virto from seeing clearly but Aragel, standing in the front, caught a fleeting view of youthful, bright blue eyes and long brown hair.

"I want to know what's happening," he said quickly. "We know about the Forest of Axter. My grandfather and father had some writings about it, but Roley and Igedian refuse to tell us anything more. There's something inside it and..."

"Go through the Great Wood to the lake and follow the river through the mountains to the Forest." Her words came out in a soft whisper, as if it was too much effort for her to say any more. The door started closing.

"Adomah!" Virto growled, squeezing past Aragel to push the door open. He grabbed Adomah by her shoulders.

"What's in there? What's in the Forest of Axter?" Adomah struggled against Virto's strong grip, and then looked up with a determined gaze. Aragel was angry and fully intended to dress Virto down when they left. He couldn't just go around treating old people like they were rag dolls that he could just shake answers out of.

"Look at yourself, you fool!" Adomah screeched. "Letting the rage use you. Shameful, pitiful! The Forest you speak of has trees that reach the heavens, and in the middle, you'll see them. The creatures sprung from Nature's bosom. But before that, you have to cross the treacherous mountains that shine with unholy light." She was speaking as if she were their oracle and sending them on this quest instead of them coming to her in search of answers.

Alarmed by the way Virto was handling Adomah, Erien rushed forward to pry Virto's fingers from her shoulders. Aragel feared his friend would harm the woman. Now free, the woman gave a wild shake of her body and laughed. "But Aragel," she said, turning to him, "You can't reach it. You don't know the dangers that lie in wait – even I don't know what they are. Nobody knows! Nobody! Nobody came back, nobody talks about what's in there… nobody… nobody…" She flung off the hood, rocking back and forth on the tip of her toes as she chanted words that were too soft to hear. Bewildered by Adomah, Aragel stared at her in a daze.

"C'mon, no use staying here now." Erien's gentle voice pulled him out of his reverie, and he followed his friends out of the cottage.

"Virto? Are you all right?" Erien said, once they had stepped out.

"Huh?" Virto frowned. He was a little dazed, and he didn't know why.

"You were a little out of it back there," Erien explained.

"I'm fine," he said curtly, turning to walk down the hill, "I'm going now. We go through the Great Wood and follow the river, right?"

"You're not going anywhere," Erien said firmly, "We don't know everything yet."

"We won't know anything if we stay here," Aragel said. "I think we should talk to Igedian again. Or Roley. Then I'll go off and search for the forest myself."

"There's no 'I' in this. Nobody is going off alone," Erien said, brows furrowing in irritation.

"You can't be serious!" Virto snarled. "I can do this on my own! What can the both of you do, huh? Hack your way to the forest?"

"I'm just saying that we need more information. We don't even know if Adomah is speaking the truth!" Aragel raised his voice defensively. It was a strange day indeed when Virto wanted nothing to do with gathering information.

"And I'm not going to wait. Any minute longer in Arya is a minute wasted!" Virto retorted.

"Will you two just shut up?" Erien barked, surprising them into silence. "Good. Now, I'm not the smartest but even I know that the two of you have been butting heads way too many times to be healthy. Virto, arguing with Aragel isn't going to make us solve... er, whatever is going on. And Aragel, you know Virto will listen if you reason things out. So, erm, yeah. Virto, you first."

Virto nodded. "What have we learned from the chest that Aragel found, and what Igedian and Adomah said? One thing is clear – the Forest of Axter exists. But what we don't know for sure is what mysterious beings are supposed to be in it, and if they'll help to remove the mysterious clouds that aren't really clouds. Still, every second counts, and if the clouds have spooked Roley that badly, I am certain that the journey has to start immediately. I can talk to people on the way and get more information from them, rather than relying on Igedian and Roley."

"All right. Aragel?"

"Since nobody knows if they are real, then it also goes to prove that they might actually exist. And the only way of knowing is for me to go to the Forest of Axter to find out," Aragel said. "And I'm going alone, because both of you have more important things to do in the village. Erien, everyone relies on your skills when it comes to repairing and making things. Virto, you are better at taking care of my Ma than I am, and I need someone reliable to do that when I'm away."

"Now it's my turn." Erien clapped his hands before

Aragel could continue, "I'm not the only blacksmith in Morenia. I'm sure they can do without me for a while." He jerked a thumb towards Virto. "And he's got a wedding to plan, so…"

"A wedding? What wedding?" Aragel asked.

"Didn't I tell? Oh right. We bumped into Roley before I could tell you about it. Virto is getting married!" Erien thumped Virto's back with a grin.

"Focus, Erien," Virto sighed. "Yes, I was going to tell you today, Aragel, before… well, before all of these things happened. Still… it can be arranged for a later date."

"No way!" Erien shook his head vehemently. "It's bad luck to keep the bride-to-be waiting. Which is why I'm going with you, Aragel. That way, there's someone to take care of your Ma, and there's someone looking out for you. It's a win-win plan!" Virto looked unconvinced and appeared to be pouting about being left behind, lips pursed, arms crossed as if trying to restrain himself. Standing opposite him, Aragel opened his mouth to protest against Erien's so-called plan. He stopped at the obstinate glint in Erien's eyes.

"OK," he said reluctantly. For now, he thought. He would find a way to shake off Erien later, and Virto, if he ended up coming along. He had to do this himself.

CHAPTER 5

Into the Great Wood

Arya was all Aragel knew. He had never thought of leaving it. The village was his home, as it had been for his forefathers who had settled in the quaint village, nestled amidst vast fields.

He touched the soft covers of his bed, feeling a mixture of unease and excitement coursing through him. He was going on a journey – just like his grandfather! After parting ways with his friends, Aragel had hurried home to work in the fields for the rest of the day. Erien had promised to meet him at the edge of the village just after midnight. Even though

Erien was one of his best friends, being alone in the fields gave him time to think, and it made Aragel wonder if he might be better off going alone.

He had just finished packing, and inside the brown cloth satchel were a few sets of clothes, two leather flasks for carrying water, a dagger, a handful of small candles, an oil lamp, unused wicks, a roll of birch-skin, ink and a quill.

He lifted up a necklace that his mother had got for him when he was ten years old. The pendant was an old chip off from a sword's hilt – he believed it might have belonged to his father or grandfather – strung on a long cord of thick leather. As a child, he had always carried it around as a good luck charm. Aragel looped it round his neck. He might not be superstitious. but he had a strong hunch that this pendant would help him on his journey. It might not have any special powers, but at least he would feel safer with it.

Aragel folded his blanket, then sat before his desk with furrowed brow. The quill wavered hesitantly over the parchment. How was he going to tell his Ma about his journey? He did not want to lie to his only family in the world. And leaving her to wonder where he'd gone wasn't going to work either. After racking his brains, he decided on a vague but hopefully reassuring message that he was leaving Arya to find something, and would return as soon as he could. It was a good thing that Virto had to stay in the village. The clever man had most likely already thought of something believable so that his Ma would not be worried sick over his disappearance.

He felt a twinge of guilt at leaving her behind, but it was for the best, he thought, blowing at the drying ink. Telling his mother where he was going would only make a mess of things. He could imagine how furious she would be if she knew that he was leaving because of the village's crazy hermit, Adomah. That would not go down well. Ma might storm over to Adomah and lecture her for hours. Aragel grinned; at least her lectures wouldn't be aimed at him for once. That made him feel a little better, too.

The candlelight flickered, sending shadows skittering across his room. He shifted the bag onto his shoulder; it was time to go. Fastening a cloak over himself, Aragel blew out the candle with a quiet huff, sending his room into darkness. He crept along the corridor and down the stairs towards the kitchen, all the while wincing at every small creak of the floorboards. It felt like an eternity had passed before he unlatched the back door to step out into the cold night.

"Thought you were lost, and in your own house too." A loud guffaw had Aragel almost tripping over his own legs in his rush to clamp one hand over Erien's mouth. He hadn't taken such pains to slip out of the house so quietly just to have his loudmouthed friend ruin everything.

"Not so loud!" He whispered urgently. "What will you do if my Ma wakes up?"

Erien stood quietly for a moment, then a broad grin stretched across his face. "She can't hear us. We're outside," Erien said, waiting for him to finish locking the back door. Aragel rolled his eyes at his friend's words.

They walked off in silence, veering away from the well-travelled paths to avoid bumping into other villagers. It would be hard to explain why he and Erien were wearing cloaks and carrying bags that were clearly meant for travelling.

"Didn't we agree on meeting at the border?" Aragel jabbed Erien's shoulder, using more force than necessary. It was as if Erien was trying to get them caught before they even left. If he hadn't wanted to come on this adventure, then he should have said something instead of sabotaging their plans. It was a good thing Erien was built like a walking, breathing mountain. He barely flinched, only rubbing at the spot with a small grimace.

"Because Virto wanted to meet me and his house was kinda nearby, so...uh..." Erien started rummaging through his massive bag, mumbling to himself while Aragel stared blankly onwards. They had met up? Without telling him? If they had already been outside the village boundary he would have given Erien a piece of his mind, but as it was, they still had to be quiet. He ground his teeth, unhappy that his friends had left him out of whatever they were planning. Or was it because he was the youngest? Aragel tensed, not listening, even as Erien continued talking and waving something in his hand.

"Then Virto said this would be useful, so – hey, you listening?" Erien's concerned face loomed into view. "Maybe we should have left in the morning. You could use the sleep."

"I'm fine," grunted Aragel. "What did Virto want with you? I thought he'd want to tag along."

"Weren't you listening at all?" Erien asked, exasperated, throwing his arms up in the air.

"I would, except that you're not telling me everything!" Aragel cried out. He'd tamped down his feeling that something wasn't quite right, and now he couldn't hold it in any more. He was frustrated that his friend thought that he had to protect him by hiding things from him.

"Heavens, just what is wrong with you, Aragel? I've been telling you what's going on and you suddenly start yelling at me!" Erien grasped Aragel's arm and pulled him along. "Now listen. I met up with Virto because he said he had something to give us, and he didn't want to interrupt you or your Ma earlier on. It's a – what's that word he used – compilation of some important clues that'd help us. Ain't a map, but it's good enough, he says. He's still not too happy about being left behind, but he agreed to watch over your Ma."

If Erien thought this little snippet of information was going to be enough to placate Aragel into being quiet and cooperative, then he had another think coming. Aragel's anger fizzled out quickly, but he wasn't going to let it go as easily. He was unable to look at Erien as the giant handed over a rolled-up parchment. Aragel stuffed it into his bag without a second look.

"Sorry. Don't know why I flared up," he admitted softly, still refusing to look at Erien. His shoulder was squeezed gently, warmth spreading in his heart as his friend accepted his apology with a warm chuckle.

"You'll feel better after we get some rest," Erien said.

While he knew that his friend was sincere, Aragel could not help feeling resentful of the comforting words. Things were not going to be as simple as that. He nodded anyway, keeping up with Erien's long strides as they approached the village's border. The boundary was marked by a stretch of dry grass with bricks piled along its length to make a rough wall. He had come here often when he was a child, dragging Erien and Virto into a make-believe world of monsters and brave warriors. It had been the perfect playground, out of sight from meddling adults, until Roley had stumbled upon them in a drunken haze. The villagers were told, and all children were banned from playing at the border. His Ma had scolded him for hours, ranting about how he should have had more sense than to play there when the bricks were old and could crumble upon them at any time.

The dirty bricks covered in twisting vines made it clear that nobody had bothered to maintain the border for a very long time. Worn down by years of wind and rain, the wall could now be scaled easily by the two young men. Aragel hefted himself onto the top, careful not to drop his bag as he hopped off the edge and landed on the other side. He took several steps before realising that his friend was not behind him. Aragel thought for a moment that this might be the best time to lose him and go out on his own. Then Erien appeared behind him.

"Think we'll be back soon?" His friend's voice sounded too loud in the sleepy silence.

"We won't if you keep dawdling like this," Aragel grumbled.

The Great Wood was just ahead. Most hunters

preferred not to go inside it, saying that there were fewer animals for them there than there were in the wide fields and sparse shrubs closer to the village. There were rumours of ghosts haunting the trees, their spirits unable to rest until they found living replacements for themselves.

Looking into the pitch-black forest, Aragel admitted to himself that it was eerie. Still, he was not going to stop just because of baseless rumours. He wasn't a child any more, and he wasn't going to let some children's horror story stop him from going into a wood.

Light shone from behind him as Erien approached. He was holding a lantern that sent shadows bouncing across trees. Aragel motioned for him to stop swinging it. "The river shouldn't be too far from here," he said.

"Let's find somewhere to turn in for the night," Erien said, "And leave the river for later. Don't want us falling into it when it's so dark. Virto said we shouldn't waste too many of our candles."

Aragel was tired, and he could really have done with a little more sleep, but he thought they should put as much distance between them and the village as they could. He didn't want to betray himself and try to go back. Although he didn't want to admit it, his friend was right. He nodded and let Erien lead the way, guided by the lantern as they searched for a suitable place to rest. They did not venture too deep into the forest. It would be troublesome if they ended up wandering too far from the river.

It took them some time, but eventually Aragel found a place to settle in for the night; the base of a large tree with roots bulging above ground. Drawing his cloak tightly around his body, he huddled against the exposed tree roots, grateful for the shield they provided against the cold night. Erien was quiet, his breathing slow and deep.

Aragel stared into the darkness, envious of his friend's ability to fall asleep despite being in a different environment. The forest was nothing like Arya; he could hear the scampering of creatures, choruses of insects chirping, an occasional beat of wings and low, mournful hoots that echoed in the night. Sighing, Aragel closed his eyes and willed himself to sleep.

***

"... but the White Knight was not fooled by the Witch's words. He waved the mighty sword and broke the mirror! The illusion was shattered and – "

"Papa! What's... ee-loo-... e-lu-sher..."

"Illusion. E-lu-shern."

"E-lu-shern... what's that?"

"It means not real. Fake. A lie. Now, can Papa

continue the story?"

"Yessir!"

"All right, where were we, hmm..."

"The e-lu-shern broke!"

"Ah, yes, yes. The White Knight, now freed from the Witch's illusion, jumped off the cliff and into the rushing rapids. He was rescued by a group of beautiful beings who lived in the forest. After hearing his plea, they decided to help him – but on one condition. He was to never reveal where he had found them, for the Witch's powers stretched far and wide, and they had been hiding from the Witch for many years. The White Knight agreed, and they slipped into the Witch's castle again. While the Witch was sleeping, they sang and danced till the Witch disappeared into the darkness, never to be seen again."

"They won!"

"Yes they did. The White Knight saved many people that day, Aragel. He was a hero."

"I wanna be a hero too!"

"Do you now? Haha! I am sure that you will be a fine hero that'll make your Ma and I very proud."

"Yes! I wanna go tell Mama!"

"Go on, then... ah, wait!"

"Papaaaaa, what is it now?"

"Aragel, what I told you... the story – yet – stop... White Knight – end... again."

"What?"

"... away – but careful – "

"I can't hear you, Papa!"

"... don't trust – forget!"

Aragel woke up with a gasp like a drowning man, arms outstretched in reach for the assurance that his Pa was there. Instead of low, musty notes that spoke of old books and ink, there was only a faint waft of dank sweat. His hands, clutching rough fabric, loosened as he took deep breaths to regain his composure.

"What happened?" Erien must have been woken by Aragel's thrashing and flailing.

"Nothing," Aragel lied, looking down at his hands. They were clammy with perspiration. He rubbed his palms. "Just a bad dream."

"About your father?" Erien knew his friend far too well. But what had given him the clue? Had he actually called out for his Pa in his sleep? Aragel nodded and busied himself with brushing dirt off the cloak.

"Let's go then. I reckon we've had enough rest for now," said Erien. Perhaps he had sensed his friend's reluctance, for he did not pursue the matter. The two friends packed up swiftly, wiping their faces and drinking several mouthfuls of water in silence. Even the forest was quiet. They trudged on, periodically stopping to scratch a tree with an 'x' so that they would be able to tell if they were walking in circles.

They had just marked the fifth tree when Aragel sensed something changing. There was not a scrap of sunlight coming in through the trees, nor was there a single patch of sky visible through the high, leafy canopy. The wood seemed to be in a state of perpetual darkness. Erien's lantern revealed vines weaving back and forth across the forest floor. The uneven growth could easily trip an unsuspecting traveller.

"I don't like this," Erien frowned. "Feels like..." He trailed off uneasily, but Aragel knew what he meant. That feeling was with him, too.

"We're being... watched?" Aragel's voice dropped at the end, suddenly conscious of how loud he sounded. Erien was silent for a moment, probably weighing his friend's response to his next words.

"Yeah. And it's too quiet around here. No birds, no creatures at all," Erien said, lifting the oil lamp to peer through the leafy branches.

"Should we try running? Might confuse whoever is following us."

"I dunno. Think we should arm ourselves first and jump the fella who's trying to spook us." Or whatever creature it might be, Aragel thought, disquieted by the idea that someone or something had caused the forest's animals to go into hiding. He followed Erien's lead, snapping off the thickest branch he could find and using his dagger to sharpen one end. It was a crude weapon, but they had little choice. With a dagger in one hand and the branch in another, Aragel felt a little more reassured. He only wished he knew what he was protecting himself from.

They made several turns, careful to keep going in the same direction – Virto's note had told them to head north-west – as they moved through the forest. At the fifth turn, Aragel stopped suddenly. He crooked his head. "I hear something moving," he whispered, trying to pinpoint the sound's direction.

Erien stopped in his tracks and nodded. He had heard the faint rustling too. They shifted till they were standing back-to-back, eyes watching the surroundings in anticipation. Neither of them called out a challenge, because neither really wanted to know what it was.

A dark brown blob streaked past Aragel, scampering up a nearby tree. Jerking back in surprise, he laughed nervously when he realised what it was. "It's only a squirrel," he said, relieved.

"At least we know what's been stalking us." Erien wiped his brow, turning to watch the little critter as it chattered at them from a high branch. They grinned at each other, the tension seeping out of their bodies. Aragel jostled Erien good-naturedly.

"Someone was afraid of a big bad scary squirrel..." But he broke off in alarm as a black shadow plummeted past Erien's hulking figure and hit the ground between them, startling Aragel into silence.

"A crow?" His friend said disbelievingly, moving the branch closer to the black shape. Frayed, black wings beat against the ground and the crow rose with a loud caw, an enraged shriek that made Aragel shrink back in shock.

"Watch out!" He pulled Erien back by his shirt just as the crow swooped towards them with another scream. They stumbled backwards, the lantern jerking out of Erien's hand as he tried to regain his balance. Perched on the edge of a tree branch, the ragged crow watched them, its small eyes glinting in the semi-darkness. Aragel lifted his dagger. He was ready to lunge against the crow when something hit the back of his head, sending black spots dancing over his vision. Loud caws suddenly reverberated from everywhere in a cacophony of flapping wings and crazed cries. Aragel felt Erien's muscles tensing under his grip. He could hardly blame his friend. A huge flock of crows was above them, blotting out the entire forest canopy. Deafening caws from behind only confirmed his suspicion; they were surrounded by the birds.

"Run!" Erien whispered. The two of them pelted through the trees, repeatedly having to fight their way clear of the vines. Aragel dashed to the left, slashing the air with his makeshift weapon and his dagger to keep the crows off. It was futile, for the birds slammed themselves against his body and face, scratching him with their sharp claws and beaks. Aragel soon found that his sharpened branch was of little use in warding off the stubborn creatures. Even after being hit, the crows continued attacking them. The two friends ran blindly, tripping over vines and exposed tree roots as they struggled to throw off their pursuers.

"Any bright ideas?" Aragel shouted.

"You tell me!" Erien tried to duck another attack, failing miserably as his size made him an easy target for the birds. Aragel, though of smaller build, was not having an easy time either. His face and arms were covered with scratches, with one exceptionally long one stretching from his left eye to his cheek. He had been lucky to stab the ferocious crow before it pecked out one of his eyes. The crows were relentless. In desperation, the two friends headed towards a denser area of undergrowth, hoping it would hinder the crows' flight. Erien, having caught up with Aragel's nimble steps, went ahead. His height enabled him to hack off the overhanging branches that were in their way.

Aragel took a moment to catch his breath and take stock of their injuries. Like him, Erien was covered with ugly gashes, his ears bleeding from the crows' attack. A loose chunk of bloodied skin the size of a thimble flapped uselessly on his right ear, and he tried to stem the blood with a corner of his shirt. It was painful to watch, so Aragel concentrated on moving his legs. They were slowing down, exhausted from running non-stop. All Aragel wanted was to get back to the safety of Arya.

"Shouldn't have gone this way," Aragel muttered. Just three strides ahead, Erien stopped and turned with a heavy scowl. "I ain't the leader round here."

"What are you trying to say?" Aragel stomped towards Erien and snatched the blood-stained shirt, throwing it onto the ground. Erien glared as he bent to pick up the shirt.

"We have no time for this," he said gruffly. The crows could catch up with them anytime. He knew it, yet just now he wanted to slam the sharpened branch against Aragel's chest, dig his dagger into his friend's shoulder and – what was he saying? Aragel was his friend. Erien's eyes widened with growing horror. What was he doing? His shoulders sagged in defeat. Just what was he thinking?

Just then a low plaintive cry rang out, its mournful pitch raising goosebumps on their skin. Another long, coarse howl answered, joining the first to form a tuneless song.

"Wolves," Erien said grimly, flinching when Aragel

turned his gaze towards him. "C'mon. I'm afraid we have very little time before they find us."

CHAPTER 6

Wolf Attack

Deep in the forest, roaring winds battered against a tall, jagged structure. It stood alone, rising above buildings surrounded by snow-capped peaks. Snowflakes floated languidly onto exposed balconies and terraces and slid downwards over icicles. Worn down but not ravaged by the chilling winds, faded gold streaks adorned banners that lay limply against the walls. The place was long empty of its occupants. In the dark interior, low creaks echoed down hallways as weakened joints protested against the onslaught of the raging winds, the structure shuddering at *unpredictable intervals. Then black swirling clouds descended. The walls rattled, and with a heavy groan, one of them crumbled, collapsing onto itself as the clouds moved as one mind.*

***

The wolves sounded close. Aragel and Erien quickened their pace, zig-zagging through the dark, dense forest in hopes of throwing off the pack. Aragel motioned for Erien to keep as quiet as possible, hoping that the crows' loud cawing would hide the sound of their footsteps. But between fleeing from their hunters and keeping up with each other, they had forgotten one crucial fact: predators rely on their sense of smell. The wolves were brutal slayers, born with a speed and viciousness that only increased during a hunt, and they were expert killers. This was a hunt, and the two friends were their prey. Aragel's breathing grew ragged. Beside him, he felt Erien inhale sharply, as if in pain.

The first wolf leaped in front of them, lips curled in a cruel sneer. A yellowed fang protruded from its upper jaw and there was a fierce squint in its eyes. It growled warningly, eyeing the long branches that Aragel and Erien were holding. Another wolf slunk towards them, its supple grey body showing off lean muscles as it joined its mate, whose name was Longfang, in circling the two. They danced gleefully around the two men, jaws snapping in a wild rhythm.

Aragel held his breath, glancing warily at the shadows darting to and fro in the trees behind the two leading wolves. It seemed as if hundreds of glowing eyes were watching their every move. How were they going to fight so many?

He sneaked a glance at Erien, finding no relief in his friend's pale face. It seemed Erien had no more idea than he did what their next course of action should be. But they could not abandon their mission so easily. They had to reach the Forest of Axter. They couldn't die here! Heroes always got happy endings. That wasn't very likely if they got eaten by wolves.

Aragel blinked rapidly at Erien, hoping that his friend would catch his silent message. He let his line of sight fall onto a large tree just a few feet away, which looked as if it could be climbed. There! He blinked again. They would have to sprint diagonally across Longfang and Greysnapper, then climb upwards as fast as they could manage before the wolves were upon them.

He looked at Erien again, silently asking his friend if he understood. This time, Erien blinked in understanding. It was now or never...

They had barely taken the first step when

threatening snarls erupted from the back. Fuelled by the instinctive need to survive, the two men ran to the tree and began to clamber upwards. It was harder than it looked; it had been a long time since they had climbed a tree, and blood kept dripping into Aragel's eye as he struggled to hold on. He was beginning to think that the wolves and the crows were working together to thwart the two of them on their mission.

Erien hoisted Aragel upwards, depositing him on one of the lower branches before pulling him up again. Slowly but steadily, they scrabbled onto the thicker branches and sat there, hugging the trunk in fear of falling down. The wolves circled them hungrily, jaws snapping in anticipation of capturing their prey.

"Well done," Erien huffed, balancing himself gingerly, "You saved our lives."

"I'm not sure about that," Aragel murmured. One wolf, Blackfoot, remained motionless, sitting at the base of the tree with its ebony fur melting into the darkness of the forest. From the way the other wolves deferred to its commanding stance with lowered tails and ears, he deduced that this one was the pack leader. Blackfoot's intelligent eyes were mocking, as if he were saying that resorting to such a foolish plan was childish. Aragel clenched his teeth. Arguing out loud with a wolf wouldn't make him any better than Adomah. He stared around him, wondering when and if the wolves would ever give up. He had got them out of a precarious situation, but the danger remained. The crows were still somewhere nearby, their caws unceasing. The two of them were covered with injuries which, while not life-threatening, hindered their movements. There was also the matter of cleaning their wounds for fear of an infection, but they didn't want to risk wasting water from their satchels. They didn't know how long they would be stuck up here in this tree. They had no way of fighting the predators, who had an extra advantage over them, being in familiar territory. Sharpened branches could be snapped easily, whereas his dagger and Erien's hammer had limited range. They could not possibly kill all the wolves with such pathetic weapons. They might maim one or two, but the remaining wolves would bury their fangs into their bodies long before another lucky strike could be placed.

Erien, who had been cleaning the rest of the blood off himself, was sullen. He was probably thinking the same thing. Neither man had joined the hunting parties when they were of age. Arya was a safe, hospitable place where the only wild beasts were the hares and deer that grazed on the village's crops. Only rambunctious fools would meet each month to venture into the nearby forests – never too far from the edge, never too foolhardy to go off alone – just to hunt for the occasional bear. The hunting party prided themselves on skilled weapons forged by Erien, brandishing fancy pitchforks and slingshots that could bring down a full-grown bear, though Aragel was sure that there was a lot more involved than that.

"We're trapped," he admitted at length.

"There must be a way out!" Erien protested.

"Unless you have a better idea, we're staying here," Aragel said, fingers tightening round the tree.

"We could... run? No? "

"Never knew you could outrun wolves and crows."

"All right, stupid idea." Aragel rolled his eyes. "What about distracting them?"

"With what?"

"Something," Erien gestured impatiently. "Anything."

Aragel made himself comfortable on the tree branch and rummaged through his bag. He had nothing that could attract the bloodthirsty beasts' attention and keep them occupied long enough to escape. Blood... if only they had slabs of meat. He rubbed against the itching scratches on his arm. Ah! That was it!

"We can do it" he said solemnly, "if we have something bloody."

"What do you – no! No way! Neither of us is going to stay behind!"

"I never said that!" Aragel said furiously. ""We just have to use ourselves as bait."

"That's crazy! Are we going to bleed to death every time we end up facing such beasts?"

They glared at each other, neither willing to back down. Aragel wanted to shout, to scream at Erien for being right. He had just wanted to get the two of them out of this dire situation, never mind the consequences. If it meant he had to lose an arm or two in exchange for their lives, he would do it.

A growl stopped Aragel from thoughts of plunging the dagger into his own arm. Blackfoot, the pack leader, was stretched out on the vine-covered ground, tongue lolling lazily as he watched the two friends squabble. The wolf looked contented. It knew it had all the time in the world. It was infuriating, and this time Aragel bared his teeth at the wretched beast.

"You're right. But we need to throw them off somehow," he said, reluctantly tearing his gaze away from Blackfoot. Any more and he might fling himself off the tree in anger. "What are you doing?"

Erien was crouching, strong hands wrapped as far around the branch as he could manage, feet inching backwards, one at a time, to balance himself. Aragel was baffled.

"I was thinking," he whispered, eyes focused on the branch, "we could use the trees, you know. To move around." The blacksmith smiled triumphantly as he pointed to the nearby foliage. "Just got to get the hang of things and we can get out of here."

"Not all the trees are close enough for that," Aragel said. It was possible, he thought, but could the branches support their weight?

"We'll have to make do with that. Crawl slowly to the end, jump to the other branch, hold on and then lift yourself up. It has to be fast. Might be better if we can make a straight jump towards the tree trunk. Then we'd have a more stable landing ground."

"Got any rope?" Erien, now reaching the branch's end, spent several seconds manoeuvring himself into a safer position. He sat up, one hand searching through his bag while his left hand reached behind for a firmer grip.

"Yeah, seven feet of rope," he said, pulling out a neatly looped coil, "and these," he tilted the opened bag to show rolls of twine. "Come on – we can do it."

* * *

An hour later, Aragel and Erien lay recovering on the grass at the edge of a lake. The seven feet of rope which had proved their saviour lay coiled up next to them. They were finally out of the forest, and the peaceful lake before them appeared untouched by any human. The sun had begun to set and small tinges of orange and pink sky could be seen. The mountains, giant and green and standing in all their majesty far beyond the lake, looked kind and gentle in the sunset, as if offering solace and protection for the night.

Deciding that the lakeside would be a safe place to rest for the night, Aragel and Erien built a small fire and laid mats on the ground to sleep on. Too tired to eat or even to talk about their adventure in the forest, they drank water from their bottles and rested their weary heads on their mats, allowing the quiet serenity of the lake to lull them into a deep sleep. Time passed...

Suddenly, standing before him, Aragel saw the strangest creature. It had the face of a human and translucent wings where its arms should have been. It stood on human legs, though its feet were like that of a bird's. With a gentle smile, it fluttered its wings gently and looked at Aragel. "Let flights of light be your guide, Aragel," it said.

"Wha... Who are you?"

"I am Danil, king of all that have wings," the creature replied, bowing its head. "You are a brave man, Aragel of Arya, and I have come to assure you that you have my honour and loyalty."

"Aragel? Wake up my brother, you're dreaming." Erien gently shook Aragel out of his slumber.

"No... what honour? Why?" Aragel was speaking in his sleep.

"Aragel!" Erien called out firmly "you're dreaming!" The sternness in his voice made Aragel snap his eyes open and stare around him.

"Oh Erien... Erien, I was dreaming and saw this creature..."

"Yes I know, you were talking in your sleep. Who's Danil?" Erien was impatient, but his eyes were full of wonder.

"I don't know... There was this creature, he was a sort of half human and I couldn't make out the rest, but he definitely wasn't all human. He had wings and there was this light all around him... oh god, it sounds so ridiculous. But it was real, Erien, I'm sure it was real. We have to find him." Erien's face fell, and he sighed heavily.

"Go back to sleep Aragel, it's just a dream," Erien replied, pulling his blanket tighter around himself. "We have a long way to go tomorrow."

But sleep would not return to Aragel. He stayed awake in the darkness to watch the waters instead. He sat silently holding his knees to his chest and watched the water. The lake was beautiful at night, like a sheet of midnight blue glass, the waters stood still and calm. The fire he and Erien made had been reduced to a smoking mound of wood and it would have been pitch dark if not for the gentle rays of a full moon reflecting its light off the lake's surface, illuminating their surroundings. Aragel could make out the towering mountains that lay before them. They looked harsher in the dark, but he still found their presence strangely comforting. The sky was filled with stars and though they relaxed Aragel's tired mind, he could not rest. Still thinking about the winged creature from his dream, Aragel sat and watched the tiny ripples that formed whenever a fish came close to the water's surface. He wondered if his mother missed him yet.

***

As dawn finally cast its warm orange glow on the horizon and Erien began to stir, Aragel had already started packing their things. The hoots of owls and the clicks of the insects had been replaced by the songs of birds which had begun their morning chorus. Unusually large forest squirrels scurried around, jumping from one tree to another. He had to look at them and smile as he recalled thinking that last night the two of them had been terrified of a squirrel. The smile faded into a frown as he recalled the real dangers that had been waiting in the night to attack them.

"I had the best sleep last night," Erien yawned. "Did you?"

"Yes I did," Aragel lied. "I must have been tired from running for my life." Erien decided to ignore the joke.

"There's something so peaceful about this place, isn't there?"

"What? Yeah sure. Where's the book?" Aragel asked distractedly.

Pulling out the ragged journal, Aragel flipped haphazardly through the pages, not quite sure what he was supposed to be looking for.

"OK here, right here. This is what we're supposed to be looking for." He said, pointing at one of the drawings in the journal.

"What is that?" Erien squinted at the drawing.

"It's a waterfall, and if I'm correct, it should be in that direction." Aragel pointed north. As Aragel and Erien packed their things, Aragel noticed that the dark cloud formations seemed lower in the sky than they had been the day before. "Were they that low yesterday?" He asked Erien.

"I don't think so." Erien looked up at the sky.

"Yeah, I don't think so either," Aragel said, hoisting his satchel onto his shoulder. "OK, we've got everything, let's go." He wanted to keep moving on their little adventure, but he couldn't shake off the fact that the clouds were nagging him. The pair walked at a steady pace, knowing they had to reach the waterfall before nightfall. The lake was as serene in the day as it had been at night. Its crystal clear waters reflected the little sunlight that shone through the dense clouds, adding a touch of hope to the dreary palette of greys and greens from the clouds and trees. The ground was hard and peppered generously with sharply-pointed pebbles, making it harder to walk, but at least the ground was not wet.

They walked along the lake, which gradually became enclosed by cliffs until it became a tree-lined ravine, a sign that they were on the right track; a good thing, since they were getting tired. It was soon noon, and their stomachs were growling.

"Here, take some," Erien offered Aragel some bread he had brought along with him.

"Thanks. You doing OK?" Aragel asked, knowing that Erien was not quite used to this much walking. He didn't know if he should tell his friend that he was happy he was there with him, because he didn't want to make Erien think he was afraid to be alone.

"I'm fine." Erien stopped. The forest had now formed a dark green canopy over them and they could hardly see the sky. All around them, giant trees more than a thousand years old stood towering over everything. Their feet ached from having walked so far and their shoulders were numb from the weight of their bags.

"Let's rest for a while," Aragel said, putting his bag down. There was a huge slab of rock with smaller rocks around it which looked like a good resting place. A modest stream flowed beside the stone, and grass provided a cushion for them to rest on. The air was still and uncomfortable, but at least it was cool and damp. It could have been much worse, hot and muggy and full of flies.

Craning his neck to look up, Aragel stood in awe, seeing how unusually tall the trees were. Their bark was thick and healthy, and their leaves, spread far and wide with the help of long skinny branches. He took a deep breath of fresh air, stretching his arms over his head and taking in the vast natural landscape lay before him.

Then suddenly he heard a rustle from behind a large boulder. "Who's there?" He snapped.

"Where?" Erien looked up.

"Did you hear that? There's something over there."

"You're imagining things, Aragel, eat something." There was a slight waver in Erien's voice, however, and it made Aragel realise that he wasn't the only one who was afraid of what might be lurking in the unknown.

"No,, I definitely heard something and it came from behind that boulder over there," Aragel replied softly, walking quietly toward the boulder. He reached it and carefully peered over it. An old man was crouched behind the boulder. His body was bare and strung loosely around his waist was a pair of tattered woven pants that reached no further than his ankles. In his hands, he held a spear that he had been sharpening on a nearby rock. He looked rather like Roley, but skinnier,

"All the better to catch fish with, you see," said the old man, acknowledging Aragel's presence. "I haven't seen you about here, from out of town are ya?" He spoke casually, as though he already considered Aragel to be his friend. "I seen you and your friend been wandering around here like lost children."

"Kind of. We're from Arya. It's a village on the other side of the forest."

"Arya, huh?" The old man looked up. Aragel couldn't be sure, but he thought there might be a hint of recognition in those old eyes.

"That's right, you know it?" Aragel said, stooping down to the old man's level.

"Know it? Yeah, I do," he replied, looking down at his spear. There was silence between them for a while as Aragel watched the old man sharpen the weapon, uncertain what to say next.

"Do you know of somewhere where we can stay for the night?" asked Aragel, finally breaking the silence.

"Unfortunately not," said the old man, a little too curt as he stood to walk towards the stream.

"Oh, you just sleep in the forest then?" Aragel asked innocently. He had the feeling that the man wasn't telling him everything he could.

"Don't get smart with me, boy," the old man grunted.

"I mean no disrespect, kind sir. It's just that dusk will be falling soon and my friend and I need to find a place to stay before we set off again. We had planned to get to... a particular spot by the time it turns dark, but it doesn't look like that's going to happen now. I promise you we will be out of your way by dawn."

"And where, may I ask, are you heading for?"

"I'm looking for another place." Aragel was deliberately being vague, because he didn't know this man and wasn't sure if he was friend or foe.

"Where is this other place?" The man tried nonchalance, but Aragel was not fooled.

"I'm afraid I cannot tell you that, sir."

"Fair enough. Have a good evening in the forest, young man," the old man replied, peering into the water, apparently looking for fish. Something told Aragel that this man could help him if he trusted him. He lowered his voice.

"The Forest of Axter," he murmured.

"What?" The old man's eyebrows shot up and he

dropped his spear. Scrambling to catch it again, he turned his attention back to Aragel.

"Axter? Whatever for?" His voice and composure were calmer this time.

"We're looking for something." Aragel furrowed his eyebrows, feeling a little challenged.

"What are you looking for there?" asked the man, resting his spear. Growing uncomfortable with the interrogation from this skinny and semi-naked old man, Aragel stood up.

"If you do not have a place to stay, sir, then that's OK," he said. "We will find a way. Good day." He turned to walk away.

"There's no way you're going to stay here tonight and wake up in one piece by dawn," said the old man.

"We'll manage," Aragel replied without turning.

That wasn't exactly what the man wanted to hear, however. "Follow me," he said, stepping out of the water.

"Thank you" said Aragel, nodding to Erien. Aragel would have rejected this offer had he not been concerned that the warning might be right. The area was foreign to the two young men and they were hungry and tired – too tired to keep watch safely during the hours of darkness. It seemed they had little choice but to trust this stranger.

The old man led them up the valley and they trudged on in silence for an hour or more. They soon began to hear the thunder of water, and not long after that they rounded some rocks to see the most magnificent waterfall Aragel had ever laid eyes upon. The sound of crashing waters was deafening and the slopes were steep and lashed with spray, but they pressed on and climbed up the damp rock, slipping every now and then. Sharp rocks were everywhere and their old guide kept a constant lookout for the two younger men; he knew that a false step could mean a nasty fall. He obviously knew the terrain like the back of his hand. He climbed ahead, tossing loose rocks aside to clear a path for Aragel and Erien. Small forest creatures peered at them from their hiding places in the rocks.

"We're here!" shouted the old man finally, struggling to be heard above the roar of the cascading waters. In front of them stood a little cottage, tucked away out of reach of the waters. "I built this myself you know. It's small, but it's cosy," he said, opening the door.

It was hard to image how this skinny old man could have managed to build this little cottage on his own. He must have had help, Aragel thought to himself as he stepped into the little home. It was just big enough for two, maybe three people, to live in. The biggest feature of the house was a small fireplace with a hand-carved mantelpiece standing over it, upon which stood some candles. Facing the fireplace, were two comfortable-looking chairs where Aragel imagined this old man would sit and spend his evenings. To the left stood a stove, a small table and three more chairs.

"Make yourselves comfortable," said their host. "Give me a moment and I'll heat some food up for us." He walked away into a small room hidden away behind the kitchenette.

Aragel and Erien made themselves comfortable in front of the fireplace while the old man heated up some food and set the table for the first proper meal they had had in days. After days of eating little but plain bread, the simple dish of beans and potatoes smelled glorious.

"So, before we eat, shall we introduce ourselves?" the old man asked, his face expressionless.

"I'm Aragel and this is Erien. We're both from the village of Arya and we are passing through these lands in search of the Forest of Axter."

"My name is Jaan and I too am from Arya."

The younger men exchanged looks of disbelief. This was a story they wanted to hear.

"Are you? Then how did you end up here?" asked Erien.

"It's a long story."

"Well we have all night," said Erien, stuffing a spoonful of beans into his mouth.

CHAPTER 7

Jaan's Cottage

"I used to live in Arya, but I was driven out," Jaan began. "My wife Adomah and I were separated when I was cast out." His voice trailed off. Jaan sighed and looked up from his bowl. His deep-set brown eyes had a look of resignation and sadness in them.

Aragel dropped his spoon.

"Adomah? Adomah the crazy lady feared by every child in Arya?"

"Adomah was my beautiful wife. She was never crazy, only misunderstood," Jaan replied sadly.

Realising how rude he was being, Aragel

apologized. "I am so sorry, Jaan, please continue."

"Adomah and I got married when we were only twenty, but we never had any children, which upset her. She longed for a child, but we simply could not conceive. We had tried every suggestion anyone offered, but ten years passed without a child and Adomah had started to become a little depressed. She became jealous of women who walked by holding their little ones, and snapped at young children when they walked by the house because she wanted to start hating children. She often cried and asked the universe why she could not be blessed with a child. When I could no longer bear to see her like that, I decided to visit the medicine woman."

"Thelia," Aragel answered, then saw that the others were staring at him. He blushed and kept his mouth shut. After all, this wasn't his story to tell.

"That's right, I went to see Thelia and she told me to return that night, for she had a suggestion that she could not risk people finding out about. When I went back, Thelia told me about the Forest of Axter. It was the first time I had ever heard of it. She said that within the forest lay some beings who could help me. Forest nymphs, she said they were called. But I had to travel to the middle of the Forest to find them. When I found them, I was to present to them gifts, gifts that symbolized purity, and then they would help me."

"So you went?" Erien asked quietly, and Aragel had to bite his cheek not to smile. Erien was wrapped up in Jaan's story, just as Aragel used to be in his father's stories.

"I had little choice. I could no longer bear to see Adomah the way she was. I returned home that night and shared Thelia's suggestion with Adomah. She feared for my safety, but her desire to conceive was so great that she decided it was the best thing to do. So I packed my things and left the very next day. I travelled through this forest as you did and through the magnificent Crystal Mountains..."

"The Crystal Mountains far beyond the waterfall?" Aragel interrupted.

"That's right, you've heard of them?"

"I've read about them," Aragel replied, walking to his satchel and pulling out the journal. "Here. This was my father's and his father's before him. They mention the Crystal Mountains here and I suppose I'm going to have to get through those too before reaching Axter."

"Who is your father?" The old man asked quietly, focusing his gaze on Aragel's face.

"Was. He passed away years ago. His name was Vaclar."

"Vaclar... Ah yes, I had heard rumours of his travels, though I never quite believed any of the stories

I had heard. I see you've inherited his adventurous spirit," Jaan said, giving Aragel a small smile of companionship.

"Yes. So tell me more about the Crystal Mountains," said Aragel, changing the subject. The pain he felt over his father's death had never diminished, and the only way he could keep himself from going under was to change the subject and keep his mind clear.

"Ah, the Crystal Mountains. A beautiful place where the trees are short and stumpy with small, hard leaves that retain water in the winter seasons. The water in the river is so clear you can fish with your bare hands and the creatures there are oddly good-natured, almost welcoming. It's a place that makes you want to stay for a long time, but they say the mountain doesn't allow people to stay for too long."

"What do you mean, doesn't allow people to stay for too long? It's a mountain, not a bed and breakfast landlady!" Erien's incredulity was easy to recognise, but Aragel knew where this was going. There were plenty of stories that he'd heard at his father's knee about inanimate objects being alive.

"I don't know, to be honest" replied Jaan. "I've only heard that people who stay in the Crystal Mountains are eventually driven out by strange things. Either that or they don't come back at all."

Aragel pondered over this for a few seconds, finding it all very odd. He wondered why something supposedly so beautiful would cause harm. Was the beauty a trap to lure people in?

"So what happened then?" said Erien, breaking the silence. He was eager to hear the rest of the story, and so was Aragel.

"Well I eventually found my way out of the Crystal Mountains and continued travelling until I reached the centre of the Forest of Axter. It's the darkest forest I have ever been in. It is a dangerous place and not for the weak-hearted."

Aragel wanted to interrupt and tell him that he begged to differ. They had come through some pretty dark and dangerous woods to get to where they were now.

"Did you find them?" Aragel leaned forward, thinking that maybe the creature in his dream had been one of these forest nymphs.

"I did. They were right where Thelia said they would be, dancing and singing. The nymphs are simple and delicate creatures with great compassion. But they are easily taken advantage of, so they are strongly protected by the Forest and the nature they live within. They rarely travel out of their home. It is said that those who make it to them are pure in heart and those who go with ill intentions are usually stopped by the Forest."

That was something that Aragel had missed in the journal. He strained his ears to catch every word.

"What do you mean, 'stopped by the Forest'?" Erien interrupted.

"I mean the Forest takes it into her hands to protect these nymphs. Nature is sensitive and delicate, Erien, it knows when there is a good or evil force within it. Often it does not intervene and lets its inhabitants do as they please, because there needs to be a balance in the Forest. But when one of her purest beings is attacked out of malice or ill intent, Nature will do whatever it can to protect them. She isn't called Mother Nature for nothing." Jaan laughed grimly at his own joke.

"Is that why the mountains feel so majestic?" asked Aragel. All through their journey through the Great Wood, he had felt as though he could sense the presence of the mountains. They felt strong and unyielding, yet Aragel felt a certain connection with them, as though he could trust them to protect him and Erien.

"You could feel that could you? Yes, if you are sensitive enough, you will be able to feel the forces of Nature around you. That night when I saw the nymphs, I felt extremely happy all of a sudden, and for no reason at all I felt like dancing and singing like them. My heart and my entire being felt so light, and I felt I never wanted to go back. But I was there for a purpose and knew I could not stay, so I presented my request to the nymphs and told them that I did not have anything to offer them except my loyalty. I even offered myself as a slave to them in return for this favour, but all they did was laugh at me as if it was the most ridiculous suggestion they had ever heard. Their laughter is like that of young children, sounding like tiny bells all around me. 'It is not needed, dear Jaan,' they said, 'we know the purity that is within you and promise to help.'

"They didn't tell me very much that night. Only that one of them would come to my house on the night of the fifth full moon. They told me to return home and prepare my house, to drape every mirror and every piece of furniture in my home with a white cloth and to make sure that both Adomah and I were dressed in white that night. They instructed me to prepare nine candles and place them in a circle on the right side of the place where I sleep, and on the left side, I was to place a garland of fresh flower buds. I made a mental note of their instructions and left reluctantly to return to Arya that night.

"When I reached home and told Adomah what had happened and what the nymphs had said, she was ecstatic and anxious all at the same time. It was nice to see her smiling and so full of hope again."

Jaan trailed off, rising out of his seat to make a hot drink. "Hot chocolate, you two?" They nodded. They were desperate to hear the rest of the story.

"Then what happened?" Aragel asked.

"We prepared the home just as the nymphs asked and at the eleventh hour on the night of the fifth full moon, a forest nymph showed up in my home just as they had promised." Jaan began to fill the kettle with water as he spoke. "She asked Adomah to lie on the bed and blew gently at the candles that were arranged next to the bed, lighting each of them with her breath alone. She then went to the other side and took the flower buds in her hand. She closed her eyes and uttered something and placed them on Adomah's stomach. She turned to me and asked me to close my eyes, then placed her hands on my chest and started chanting something. When I opened my eyes, I saw that the flower buds had bloomed into their full beauty."

"She did magic on you?" asked Aragel. Magic was rarely heard of in Arya and those who spoke of it were usually deemed to be evil and impure in heart. He needed to hear that someone who wasn't considered crazy by the town had experienced this, too.

"Every human being is a balance of good and bad, purity and evil, just as the universe is. Because an unborn child is yet to be touched by anything of the world as we know it, while it is within its mother's womb, it is still fully pure. Therefore, in order to make the child, purity is needed," said Jaan.

"So you're telling me that the forest nymphs somehow impregnated Adomah by chanting something?" Erien asked, incredulous. Aragel could see him gearing up for an argument.

"Don't be stupid, Erien. We had to do what everyone does to have children. All the nymphs did was to purify Adomah and me and make Adomah's body receptive to bearing children."

Aragel did his best to smother his laughter.

"OK.... so Adomah became with child that night?" said Erien, unable to hide his disbelief. Aragel's gaze stayed fixed on Jaan.

"That's right, she did," Jaan smiled cheekily. He had left out the details, but Aragel could see by the look on his face that that night had been special for the two of them.

"Why did you get cast out then?" Aragel asked, reaching for the hot chocolate; the excitement of the story had left his mouth dry.

"Well," Jaan sighed, clasping his hands. "One day, my friend Lazar came to ask me how Adomah came to conceive. He wanted to know because he and his wife Agnessa were having the same problem. It took me a long while to decide whether or not to tell him, but I eventually did because I felt bad for them. I didn't expect him to tell anyone. I had told Lazar in confidence but should have known that he'd ask people around him for advice. He never was a strong character, that Lazar. Eventually the whole village came to know and of course by then, the story had a few variations. People did not think much of it at first and thought I was making things up. Sometimes they'd make fun of me when they saw me; they thought I was making up stories to get attention. Lazar however had taken me seriously and made his journey into the Forest without telling anyone.

"It was only when Agnessa became worried when Lazar had not returned that she started telling people what had happened. People started blaming me for planting ideas in Lazar's mind, saying I should have known better than to tell such stories when they were both so vulnerable. 'It's his fault,' they would say when they saw me in the fields. They thought I had dealt with dark magic because they believed the Forest to be evil and assumed that whoever could withstand it must be evil himself. Eventually Adomah decided it was getting too dangerous for me to stay in Arya and sent me away. She was afraid that if they came for me, she and the baby would also be taken."

"Why didn't Adomah go with you?"

"She couldn't, she was still pregnant with our baby and the journey would have been too dangerous for her." A silent tear ran down Jaan's cheek, and Aragel had the decency to look away while the old man wiped it off. Erien, on the other hand, had never been so sensitive and carried on staring at their host.

"Did you ever get to see her again?" asked Erien.

"Yes I did. I would creep back into the village when it got dark every now and then to visit her. I would always make sure no one saw me."

"But I've never seen Adomah with a baby," said Aragel.

"Word was going around about our baby, that maybe it too would be evil since it was my child too, and Adomah began to worry about the child's safety. On one of the nights I had crept in to see her, she told me she feared for the life of our unborn child and asked me to return as soon as it was born. At that time, she was almost ready for childbirth and we both knew it would be just two or three more days before she went into labour. When I returned, seven nights had passed from the time our child was born, and it was then that I took him and brought him away." Jaan gave a strangled sob, and Aragel could feel his own emotions welling up.

"Then where is...?" but Aragel was interrupted by a small voice that called out from a small room behind the kitchenette: "Papa, I'm hungry!"

"I'm here, Gavril," called Jaan, smiling and rising from his chair. "He's right here with me," he said to Aragel and Erien. "Come out and say hello to our visitors, son."

A small boy came into the room. "Who are these people, Papa?" he asked, eyeing Aragel and Erien cautiously.

"They're travellers I met while I was fishing. They'll stay here for the night."

"Why?" A little petulance crept into the child's voice.

"Because they don't have anywhere else to go," said Jaan.

"Where're you from?" said Gavril, turning to Aragel and catching him off guard.

"We come from Arya, a village not too far away from here," said Aragel, slightly taken aback by Gavril's sudden forwardness.

"There's where Mama stays! Right Papa?" The child's face was instantly transformed with love and happiness. These people had to be good people if they knew his mother.

"That's right, son."

"Then why can't they go back there, Papa, why do they have to stay here?" asked Gavril innocently.

"They're staying for the night because they're

travelling somewhere else tomorrow," said Jaan kindly. "That's enough questions for tonight, kiddo. Come and help Papa prepare beds for them."

Outside, the sky had turned darker and the usual choir of insects had begun its chorus of night songs again, but there were no other animals about. Aragel had stepped outside for some fresh air. Even the sounds of the insects seemed a little more solemn than they had the night before. Through the little round window that looked into the cottage, Aragel watched Jaan and Gavril play-fighting as they prepared a comfortable space for their guests to rest in for the night. Feeling a gentle warmth spreading through his chest as he watched father and son playing with one another, Aragel wondered if Arya would ever feel the warmth of sunlight again. The reason for this journey was suddenly coming back, and it was causing him more and more worry as the days went by.

CHAPTER 8

Aragel Alone

Erien tapped on the window, signalling to Aragel that their beds were ready. Suddenly realising how cold it had become, Aragel blew into his hands and stepped back into the warmth of the cottage, his heart heavy and his hands cold.

Erien dozed off fairly quickly and his breathing had progressed into a gentle snore, but Aragel was unable to sleep. Hel draped himself in his thick woollen blanket and crept out of the house. The sky was still possessed by the dark grey clouds, but now they revealed a sliver of midnight blue sky just above the cottage. Finding a ladder leaning against the cottage, Aragel climbed it and sat comfortably on the thatched rooftop.

Thoughts buzzing with the journey ahead, Aragel began to have doubts over whether it was a journey that really required two people. To him, this journey was personal, a journey he felt he should make alone, though he could not quite put his finger on the reason why. For reasons unknown to him, every time he looked at Erien, a feeling of sadness washed over him and he felt he should leave him behind and make the journey alone. He was grateful for his best friend's company and could not bear to hurt him, but there again, he thought it would be beneficial for his mother if Erien was around to look after her in Arya. If Erien went back home, at least Aragel could journey on knowing his mother was in good hands. Though he trusted Erien with his life and there was no one else he would rather go on this journey with, something kept nagging at him to take the journey alone.

He stared up at a lonely star shining through the dark clouds and made his final decision. He would continue alone. He knew Erien would understand; he had to.

***

"Gone? What do you mean he's gone?" Erien raged. He

couldn't believe that Aragel would just leave him alone with strangers in a strange place. That was so unlike him, especially after all the dangers that the two of them had faced together so far.

"He must have left early this morning," said Jaan, indicating the neatly folded blanket on the armchair.

"You're joking. He can't have left me here by myself!"

"You're not alone, I'm here," said Jaan nonchalantly. "Besides it's not as if he left without saying anything; he explained everything in this." He handed Erien a note Aragel had written the night before. It explained why he had to take the journey alone and pleaded for Erien to understand why. It also asked him to take care of his mother when he returned to Arya. He had signed off by wishing him a safe journey and requesting that Jaan make the journey back with Erien, since he was well acquainted with the route.

"We need to leave first thing tomorrow morning if we're going to reach the first safe rest point by nightfall," Jaan said, holding out a plate of warm bread. "It's too late to leave now. Come, have some breakfast."

A mixture of emotions was warring within Erien. He was furious with Aragel for leaving him like that, but knew his presence back at Arya would bring great comfort to Cyrella. He worried for Aragel's safety and wondered if Aragel would be able to survive the journey alone. Ignoring Jaan's offer of breakfast, he walked over to his bag and rummaged through it.

"Wily fox," Erien muttered. Aragel had taken the rope, one water bottle and all the bread Erien had kept in his bag.

"He probably knew you wouldn't need any of that stuff, since you're here" said Jaan, breaking into Erien's thoughts. "It's for the best. Come, eat something and then you can help me prepare for the journey back tomorrow. Gavril's coming with us, so we need to make sure we pack everything for the safest journey."

Erien didn't think it would be safe to bring a child along on the trip, but he couldn't very well stay there all alone either.

***

Finally alone and on a path less trodden, Aragel pulled out some bread from his bag and munched while he walked uphill towards the peak of the waterfall. It was steep in some places and gently sloping in others. The terrain was bleak, hard and rocky as it had been the entire way, but the view made up for it. All around Aragel, below him, beside him and above him, stood trees in different shades of green.

His thoughts drifted back to the journal he had found and the route he should be taking. Looking over to his left, a steep drop revealed a rushing river brimming with jagged rocks and boulders. He had only the dagger he had found in his father's room to keep him safe, a compass and the trusty, raggedy journal to guide him through the days until he reached the Forest of Axter. The roads were daunting, and though he was now free to do as he pleased, the burden of being alone was a heavy one.

Finishing the bread, he checked to see how much more he had left before he had to start hunting for food. There should be enough for him to travel on for several more days. The only problem was that he had no idea how long it would take for him to get to the Forrest.

The further he walked, the heavier his heart grew as the reality of being alone weighed down on him. Trees with long, lanky branches arched above him, connecting in a sort of leafy archway that sheltered him from whatever sunlight would have shone on him. He could no longer tell what time of the day it was, and he knew that was something he quickly had to learn so that he would know how fast he needed to travel to find safe places before nightfall.

With water cascading thunderously down on his left and giant towering trees to his right, Aragel had little room for error. The air was misty and cold, a far cry from the warm breezes of Arya, and it was getting ever colder as he climbed higher. He had to stop every now and then to get acclimatised to the thin, cold air. Although it was still daylight, it felt like dusk.

Looking up at the boughs arching overhead, Aragel noticed that their surfaces were becoming darker. They also seemed to have a glossy sheen to them, as though there was something sticking to them. There were no leaves on the branches, only what seemed to be tiny little thorns. Curious, Aragel reached out to touch the surface and a tiny spike pricked his index finger, drawing blood. He instinctively stuck his finger in his mouth, then, realising the thorns might be poisonous, spat out the bloodstained saliva.

His fear growing in the dim light, Aragel picked up his pace, talking to himself as he went along to keep his mind from wandering too far. He talked to the trees and the path beneath him, asking them to guide his way and keep him safe. He received little reassurance, stumbling instead every now and then on the rough stony ground and keeping as close as possible to the right.

He was beginning to fear that maybe travelling alone was a bad idea. After stumbling over a rock for the umpteenth time, he decided to stop for a rest. He sat himself down on the ground, wondering what more the road ahead had in store for him. The ground was dry, yet moss grew on the stones, making it slippery. The air was still and dead and no sign of life was to be seen anywhere. Even the trees did not look alive with their glossy black bark.

He took a deep breath and stared out into the distance. Past the massive trees, Aragel suddenly realised he could see plumes of smoke and distant rooftops. A village! The smoke must be coming from the chimneys of people's houses. It had been only hours since he had left Erien and Jaan, but he already missed the company of other people. He had a direction now, thought Aragel to himself. The town was grey and sombre-looking, but at least there would be people there, people he could talk to and who might give him food and sustenance.

BOOM! A sudden blast of thunder struck, shocking Aragel, who instinctively put his hands over his head. *Please tell me it's not going to rain*, he thought. But then, as though Mother Nature thought it would be highly entertaining to see a young man scramble for shelter in the worst possible place, it started pouring. Finding a small patch of shelter beneath a particularly thick branch, Aragel huddled under it and pulled out the dagger he had found in his father's room. Tracing the blade with his finger, he thought about Erien and everyone back home. He didn't know if he would ever see any of them again, and the thought filled him with sadness. Pressing the point of the dagger into the face of the tree bark, he started to carve the letter A. He looked ahead of himself as he carved, thinking maybe he should do this at intervals along his way so that his path would be marked.

***

Back at Jaan's house, Erien stuffed a blanket as far down into the bag as it could go. "I think that's enough stuff, Jaan," he said, looking at the giant bag of things Jaan had packed for the trip back to Arya. It was almost the size of the little boy.

"You roll your eyes now, but you'll soon see we need this stuff," replied Jaan. "We're travelling at daybreak so that we can get there by nightfall. There will be two periods when we find ourselves in darkness. It's not just you and me on this journey, we have a child coming with us, and that my friend, is when things get a little heavier and a little bit more complicated."

Erien bit his tongue. He wanted to tell Jaan very sarcastically that he was beginning to see that.

"I wonder how Aragel is," said Erien.

"Probably wet. It's pouring," said Jaan, looking out the window. Erien didn't know what was wrong with him, but a large portion of him wanted to laugh at that. Maybe it made him feel a little justified, because he felt that Aragel had abandoned him.

"Yeah, probably regretting he left me behind now," said Erien resentfully.

"Don't think so highly of yourself, young man. He probably did what he thought was best," said Jaan, tossing Erien a water bottle. Feeling thoroughly chastised, Erien frowned as he looked back out the window. He hoped that Aragel was OK. He didn't want anything to happen to him, honestly he didn't; he was just hurt that he'd been left behind. He said a quick prayer for his friend's wellbeing.

"Aragel isn't the strongest guy in town, he acts on a whim and never considers the dangers around him," he said. "He almost got us killed out there because he thought it'd be a fantastic idea to lure the wolves away with his blood." He felt he had to explain to Jaan what kind of a person he was so that he would understand the sarcastic humour with which the friends abused each other.

"Well, there's no use in pondering over what he is and isn't. Besides, wanting to use himself as bait says a lot about his loyalty towards you. There's nothing we can do about it unless we go looking for him, and that's just asking for trouble. Stop punishing yourself over it and focus on getting back. You're going to have to explain a lot of things to Cyrella, from the sound of things."

That last statement brought Erien back to the present. He hadn't even begun to think about what he would tell Aragel's mother, and now he cringed at the mere thought.

"Aunty Cyrella! She's going to be so worried that Aragel's on his own now. At least if I was with him, she'd be assured. Virto is there with her, he would have been able to take care of her. Why do I have to do it?" But then, realising he was beginning to sound like a child, Erien snapped his mouth shut.

"Well, he must have thought something of you," said Jaan.

"Or nothing, to have left me behind," said Erien. The two of them could have gone on for a long time, as Erien was stubborn once he got into an argument, but Jaan knew he had to nip it in the bud before it could get that far.

"Oh stop it! Listen, he must have thought something of you to want you to take care of his mother. He must have left on his own for a reason, and I'm sure that whatever that reason was and whether he was acting rashly or not, it was for the best. Aragel is intuitive, I see it in his eyes. He might not understand why he feels the things he does or why he ends up doing them even, but he follows his heart and he knows within him what the best thing to do is, and so it will be. So stop whining and finish this packing.

I'll have to run you through the route after this and we need to get an early night if we're going to leave early."

Erien looked at his bag with resentment settling deep within his heart. He missed his best friend and he still could not quite accept that he would have left him alone. He was worried, but knew there was little he could do. Burly as he was, the truth was that Erien was scared to go on his own. He had been shaken by everything that had happened so far; he did not think the journey would have been this hard. The last thing he needed was to be alone with no water, food or shelter. In that sense, Aragel was the braver of the two of them. Ever since they were children, Aragel had always been the first to climb tall trees or jump across rushing rivers. He was the one who knew no danger, and when he did, he always felt determined to overcome it. Erien would only follow suit after being assured by Aragel that it was safe. Aragel was his strength, and Erien knew he would not make it one night out there without him.

***

Night had fallen by the time the storm had passed. The ground was moist and the smell of wet earth and grass was refreshing. Aragel had managed to get through the downpour without getting drenched and he had finished carving an A as it stopped.

He walked further up the path and came to a small cave in which he decided he would spend the night before leaving for the little group of houses he had seen. Tomorrow, he decided, would be a good day, and he would discover the next step of his journey.

Finding a comfortable spot, he curled himself up and pulled his cloak tightly about himself to keep warm. The night was quiet and still. There were no sounds, no insects, no animals, no living creatures to be heard or seen. It was as if Aragel was completely alone in the entire world. He soon drifted off to sleep.

It was still dark when Aragel began to stir. With his eyes barely open and drifting in and out of sleep, he thought he saw a shadow flicker past in front of him.

CHAPTER 9

The Walled City

Beyond the trees where the little houses stood billowing smoke, the city of Malur sat quietly tucked in between the tallest mountains anyone ever saw. In the far north of the city, towering over everything else, was a tower upon which lay a curse, inflicted by the Raggotah when it had ravaged Malur. Souls that had sold themselves to the Raggotah seeped in and out of the tower as it pierced the dark clouds.

Years before, the Raggotah had invaded Malur. As it was filled with debauchery and the works of the wicked, it did not take long for the Raggotah to gain control. The people of the city were greedy and were easily taken in by bribes of material gain. Somehow, in time, the more people wanted, the more they had to give up. Before they realised it, they had sold their souls and lived at the mercy of the Raggotah. Unseen by anyone, the Raggotah gained power through the pathetic souls of the people of Malur and had even slowly begun to change the geography of the mountain range. From a bird's eye view, if you looked closely, you would be able to make out the sinister shape of a snake, its head being the city with the tower standing strategically where the eye of the cobra would be. Sharply-pointed rocks and thorny rose bushes covered the city, and a wall of black and grey solid rock, created to block both man and the dead from leaving, stood on its outermost circumference.

Uncertain what the strange shadow was and not sure he wanted to find out, Aragel squeezed his eyes to make sure they were shut. He was not even sure if he was still sleeping or had really seen something. Remembering that he was now alone, he decided to wake up and keep himself occupied. He unscrewed the cap of his bottle and took a gulp, then poured some water out on his hands and rubbed it over his face to freshen himself up. He had little choice, since there was no water around him. Soon this water would run out and he would have to find a new source. He had doubts about drinking rainwater, for who could tell what the water now held within it. No matter how much it rained, the clouds still remained thick and dark, and it didn't make sense to drink from such a dubious source. Then again, he might find himself with no choice.

He pulled out some bread and took a bite, thinking about how he had stolen it from Erien just the night before. He missed him dearly and wished he had not had to leave him behind. It was an act that he himself did not understand. Why could Erien and Virto not follow him? Why did he keep sensing that this was something he had to do alone? Why did he sometimes feel he was being protected and other times as though something evil was watching him?

A thousand questions pummelled his mind, until finally he could take no more and stood up. It was time to walk on to the house below, where perhaps there would be answers for him.

He travelled for many hours, and the scenery changed as he walked along the stony path. In certain places, the arches above him had a bluish-grey tinge that made him feel comforted and safe. In other places, they were the glossy black he had seen earlier in his journey. His feet had started to ache as he trudged along, stopping to mark a tree with a carved A every so often. Keeping his mind full of thoughts of his mother and his loved ones back in Arya, he sang songs of his childhood to himself to keep his mind entertained, occasionally bursting out into chorus and breaking the still wilderness. He tried to see how far his voice could reach before it echoed back at him. If there were animals along the way, even dangerous animals, there would be some excitement. But there were none, and Aragel's own voice was all he had for company.

He walked mindlessly, swiping his dagger randomly at the branches that hung lower than the rest. Sometimes he would pretend that they were dangerous creatures he had to fight off.

Caught up in his fantasy world, Aragel hardly noticed when he had arrived at the crossroads of the arches. To his left lay dead, barren land with the occasional yellow-leafed tree peppering the grey and stark space. He had seen similar trees in Arya, but none of them had been quite so dull and dry. In the distance stood huge caves with pointed entrances, nothing like he had ever seen before. The inverted triangular shapes of the entrances were remarkably symmetrical, almost as if someone had measured them before building them. They were however, naturally formed, almost as though an earthquake had once shaken the ground and pushed the earth upwards to form these formidable structures.

To his right stood the settlement he had seen from a distance, the city of Malur, though Aragel did not know yet what it was called. He stood for a long while, considering which way he should go, eyeing each area carefully and staring far out into each path to see if he could detect any danger.

Both paths looked equally dark and dangerous, and both seemed to have an ominous air to them. He finally decided to walk towards the town because, despite its dreary grey and brown appearance, it would at least have people living there and maybe someone there could give him guidance in his journey. There was no telling what would be in the caves, for he could not see past their black mouths and he was not about to go wandering into them alone.

He walked on until he was closer to the city. From a short distance, he saw that a huge wall stood between him and the rooftops with the smoking chimneys, with no sign of an entrance anywhere. He walked along the wall, running his fingers along the walls, which were curiously ice-cold. He was increasingly aware that despite having found some form of civilization, his heart felt heavy. He felt sad and filled with sorrow for reasons unknown to him. It was almost as if this place refused to allow him to be happy.

He shuddered at the cold and pulled his cloak

tighter around him. At least his thick boots kept his feet warm, though he noticed that they had stiffened quickly in the cold. How strange all of this was, given that just a few moments before beads of sweat had been trickling down his face.

Aragel called out, hoping that someone would hear him and maybe offer to take him in and provide him with refuge for the night that was drawing close, but there was no answer. He called again, until his throat was dry. His hopes slowly dwindling, he walked faster along the endless wall. He had no idea how big the city was – for clearly it was a large city – or how long these walls stretched for; he might end up walking for hours.

With a sigh of frustration, Aragel stopped and took a step back from the wall, inspecting its width. About ten feet from where he stood, he noticed a thin vertical crack along the wall that ran from its uppermost edge to the ground. Walking slowly towards it, Aragel realised that it was an entrance; or at least it seemed like one. It was a long thin opening which ran from top to bottom, no wider than two feet.

Sliding his slim frame through the crack, Aragel took care to be discreet. Smoke and dust blew into his eyes the moment he set foot into the city, blinding him momentarily and bringing tears to his eyes. When he had wiped away the dust and the tears, he saw before him a house with peeling walls and broken windows.

The ground looked charred, burnt straw lay strewn all over the place and there was an overpowering stench of ammonia and something worse; burning flesh. A fine greyish dust seemed to coat everything in sight; doorsteps, rooftops, everything. A horse-drawn carriage stood abandoned, and a tired-looking horse chewed on scraps of straw beside it.

In the centre, between the houses, there was a stone structure in the shape of a giant tree. It looked like the trees Aragel had seen on the path to the city. Surrounding it were houses and shops, all with the same dull grey walls. There was no colour to this place and Aragel was starting to feel uncomfortable. Though some houses seemed to have smoke coming out of their chimneys, not a single soul was in sight.

Except one. On the step of one house, a worn-out looking man sat covered in grey dust, his head leaning against the door frame.

"Hello sir?" Aragel called out. The man did not answer, so Aragel decided to walk up to him. "Hello sir?" He said again. Once again, there was no answer. "Hello?" Aragel called one last time, reaching out this time to shake the man. He recoiled in shock. The moment Aragel shook him, the air was filled with grey dust, revealing a decomposing body. Ash - the entire place was covered with ash. Where had it all come from?

Suddenly terrible images began to fill his mind - people being burned at the stake, strange cult rituals and masked men on horses rampaging through the city.

"You're not from Malur, are you?" A small voice called out from behind him. Aragel swung around to see a young girl, no more than ten years old, standing behind him. She wore a worn-out blue cotton dress that had a little yellow flower pattern on the corner. Her curly blonde hair, tied loosely into a single braid, sat on her left shoulder. She was the only splash of colour against the dreary grey scene around them.

"No I'm not," said Aragel, walking towards the little girl and stooping to eye level. "How did you know?"

"Nobody from here ever touches the lost," said the little girl.

"Who are the lost?"

"The ones who gave up their souls. They're called the lost because they never found their way back," replied the little girl. She was speaking in riddles, and Aragel had no idea what she meant.

"What do you mean?" said Aragel. His voice lowered to a whisper. "Are they dead?"

"Yeah, I guess you could say that. They make for a good fire though," said the little girl casually.

"Why's he just lying there then? Why didn't

someone take him away or bury him? Wait, did you say they make for a good *fire*?" He was incredulous at what he thought he'd just heard. Surely he was misunderstanding the little girl. She couldn't be that cruel?

"You ask a lot of questions for a big person, mister. I'm just a little girl. If you don't know why, how am I supposed to know?" she shrugged. "I have to go now," she said walking away.

"Where are you going?" Aragel asked.

"Home. I'm late," she replied, breaking into a run and disappearing down the misty path in between two houses.

"What's going on?" he muttered to himself. 'Wait!" But she had gone, leaving nothing but the smoky air. He walked quickly towards the direction she had run in and saw that the pathway led to what looked like the centre of the city. So that was where the smell of burning flesh was coming from..

***

The centre of the city was nothing like the outskirts; there was life there. A group of men sat around on stone benches chatting over beer, women hanging off their arms. Aragel recognised their armour and knew they were knights. Long ago when he was still a child, his father would bring him up to the highest point in Arya to show him what lay around them. On these occasions Aragel would sometimes see a knight riding through the forest or down one of the mountain paths. He never knew where they were going or where they came from, but now he realised they must have been coming from Malur.

The roadway was cobbled, and horses stood around with their heads hanging down and carriages harnessed to their backs. People selling vegetables and fruit sat outside or in their little shops watching people going by with expressionless and empty eyes. Dark staircases from the shops led up to the living quarters where Aragel guessed the shopkeepers and their families must live. He guessed that it was probably where the smoke came from too, and just as he had the thought, he looked up and saw high chimneys blowing out thick grey smoke. He shuddered again at the thought of burning flesh. The smell was not as bad here though, he noticed.

Under the vacant stares of the city folk Aragel was getting increasingly uncomfortable and rather nervous, yet he could not help staring at the succulent fruit laid outside the stores in all its colourful glory. He had missed the taste of fresh food and longed for a bite of a crunchy red apple or a juicy pear. But he was afraid to stop and speak to these hostile-looking people. Instead he tried to avoid eye contact, fearing someone would ask him where he was from or where he was going. At this point, he was not ready to be caught off guard with any sort of interrogation and wanted to be left alone until he was more sure of himself. He walked on as though he knew where he was going and looked only at the path ahead of him, though he could not resist occasionally glancing at a store just to see what it was selling.

"Ouf!" he exclaimed, his hand flying to the back of his neck. Something hard had hit him. He turned around and saw a chubby old woman in a tattered red dress staring at him. He looked around to see if anyone else had seen what had happened, but everyone seemed to have gone back to whatever they had been doing before. He looked again at the old woman. This time she beckoned him with one arm, but her expressionless face intimidated him, so he turned away and continued along his way. He had seen what looked like a cathedral up ahead and thought that maybe he would find someone there who could help him.

Absorbed in his thoughts, he continued walking, but as he moved off he felt a hand grab his arm. It was the old woman again. Up close, it was clear she had not had a shower in days. Her dark auburn hair was unkempt and held back with a bonnet. Soot stained her face and her fingernails, but her eyes were kind and gentle.

In her hands she held two large apples, which she held silently out to Aragel. He was uncertain about the intentions of this old woman, but not wanting to be rude, he accepted the apples and placed them in his pockets. He held her gaze for a few moments and uttered a soft "thank you" before starting to walk away again, but the old lady grasped his hands suddenly, holding him back.

"You will help Malur," she said. It was not a question, more of a statement, as if she knew something about the future that Aragel did not.

"Who is Malur?" asked Aragel. The woman's face broke into a grin and she let out a loud laugh.

"Malur!" she said, spreading her arms out to indicate the city around them.

"This place is Malur?" asked Aragel.

"Yes, yes. This is our city." The woman nodded, her eyes sparkling. Sensing people were beginning to take notice of this odd exchange between the young man and the old woman, she beckoned Aragel into her shop, pretending she was trying to get him to buy fruit from her. It was a damp, cold place, but it was obvious that she had made efforts to make it comfortable. Fruit of various kinds was piled up against the walls, leaving a circular space in the middle of the room. A little round table stood above a bright yellow rug and an oil lamp in the middle of the table softly illuminated the shop. Aragel looked at the strange old woman, trying to anticipate what she might want to tell him.

"This place name Malur," she started in broken English. "You from where?"

"Arya," Aragel replied cautiously.

"Ah... Arya!" the woman exclaimed. Aragel wondered where she was from, for her speech was strange.

"I from Malur," she said. "No much English in Malur when I am young girl. People speak old language of Malur here. Malur old village, used be a nice place."

"Yeah, it looks like a lovely place," Aragel replied sarcastically.

"Yes, beautiful place!" she said sharply. "Only bad things happen that make Malur change."

"What changed? What happened?"

"You cannot stay here long time. They are watching." She looked around her shop as if she expected someone to come bursting through her walls at any moment.

"Who's watching?" asked Aragel.

"They is watching," the woman said, taking Aragel's hands and looking intently into his eyes as if she wanted him to read her mind. "Where you going?"

she said, changing the subject.

"I am on my way to the Forest of Axter."

"Axter!" the woman said in surprise, dropping Aragel's hands as if they were on fire.

"Uh, yes ma'am. I was on my way to Axter but I saw this city from a distance and decided to make my way here. I thought maybe someone here would help me and give me refuge until I find my way again."

The woman spun around suddenly and began to shove more fruit into his hand. "You take more," she said.

Aragel laughed at her odd behaviour, but suddenly he felt almost as though he was back with his mother in Arya. He missed his home, and he was tired. He needed a place to rest for the night, a warm and comfortable place, like this little shop...

"You go now," the old woman said, breaking Aragel out of his thoughts and disappointing him. He had been hoping this kind old woman would let him stay in her cosy little shop-house until he was ready to go on his way again. She ushered him out the door, dropping more fruit into his bag, and waved him off in the direction he had come from. As Aragel walked away, he took a huge bite out of an apple, savouring the sweet crunchiness of the red fruit.

The nearer he came to the cathedral, the warmer he began to feel. A beautiful structure of stone and stained glass, it stood majestically amidst the grey village. There was no traditional cross on top of the cathedral, something Aragel found rather strange, for he had never seen a cathedral without a cross before.

He walked through the tall, white, elaborate gates of the cathedral and saw the most mystical courtyard he had ever seen. Candles of every size placed on pillar-like stone structures no taller than Aragel lined the pathway toward the main hall, their little lights flickering like fireflies. Tents peppered the cathedral courtyard, and people went about their daily activities. People spoke in low voices and the atmosphere here was quite different; it was more peaceful and the air was warmer and lighter. People pumped water at the pumps in the corners of the courtyard and children ran around playing games, their laughter like music in Aragel's ears.

Aragel stood and gazed at the people of the village for a while. He noticed a beautiful dark-haired girl standing at the entrance of the hall. She had been watching over some children playing and she looked up as Aragel walked in. From where he stood, Aragel could see little yellow flowers in her hair and the soft features of her face. She had a certain glow to her, with her cheeks slightly flushed pink and eyes the shape of almonds. Her white dress fluttered gently in the warm breeze.

Aragel stood and watched her for a while until she

finally took notice of his gaze and smiled. Aragel nodded in acknowledgement and walked up to her. She seemed friendly; maybe she could tell Aragel a little bit more about Malur and maybe even know someone who could offer him a rest for the night.

CHAPTER 10

Katharina

"Hi, I'm Aragel," he said, bowing slightly.

"Katharina," the girl replied with a shy smile.

"Are you from here?" Aragel asked.

"Yes, I am. You're obviously not," said Katharina as she studied Aragel, taking in his black, dusty jacket and brown pants with many pockets. "You look a little too modern for old-fashioned Malur," she explained. Aragel smiled. The connection was almost immediate, and he instinctively knew he could trust this girl.

"I was wondering if you could help me to find some place to rest for the night," he said. "And maybe someone who could tell me how to get to the Forest of Axter?"

Her eyes widened for a split second. "Axter?"

"Yes, why do I keep getting that reaction here?" said Aragel. He was beginning to get annoyed with it, but he didn't want to say that and ruin his chances of getting the information he needed.

Katharina shrugged. "Axter is dangerous," she said. "No one normally wanders into it because it's so thickly wooded, and they say it is full of evil."

She turned and began to lead him through the cathedral, telling Aragel of some of the stories she had heard about the Forest of Axter as a child and the rumours that went around in Malur about the evil beings there. They explained that whoever went into the forest never came back out again. She spoke with a certain enthusiasm, which amused Aragel.

It was certainly a spectacular building. Giant floor-to-ceiling candles stood like pillars everywhere, taking Aragel's breath away. Simple wooden pews lined the place and stained-glass windows high above the pews depicted the life of Jesus. The glass ceiling was high and opened up in certain places to allow air to flow through, and the walls, painted white, had a strange whimsical pattern on them. Everything was ornate.

"Are you listening to me?" He suddenly heard Katharina say.

"What? Yes, yes of course I have been listening. You were talking about the evil in Axter and about people wandering through the forest and coming back strange," said Aragel, still staring around the cathedral, running his fingers over the hand-carved pews.

Katharina rolled her eyes impatiently. "I said they never come back, not they come back strange. You're not listening, and if you're not going to listen to what I have to say then there's really no point in me helping you." She crossed her arms over her chest.

"No! No, please go on," said Aragel, recovering from his amazement. "I'm sorry, this place is just so beautiful, I have never seen anything like it before. It's so carefully put together, as if everything has a purpose for being exactly where it is."

"That's because that is exactly how it was meant to be" replied Katharina. "So, as I was saying. Many hunters have wandered into the Forest of Axter because they hear stories about the game there and it became a sort of competition over who could bring back the best game from Axter. But for some reason, whoever ventured in there never came back. It's creepy really."

Aragel appreciated having someone talk his ear off again. He missed so many things about home; this was a relief and it took his mind off things. It helped that

Katharina was nice to look at as well. She had an aura about her that attracted him and made him feel comfortable immediately.

Just then a middle-aged man walked up to them. "I'm sorry, I couldn't help but overhear you speak of Axter," he said. "Are you planning to go to Axter, Katharina? Do your parents know about this?"

Katharina looked at the man and let out a tinkle of laughter.

"Oh don't be silly, Uncle Honza! I would never go into Axter. I'm only telling this young man here all about the stories I've heard about it. He's planning to journey there tomorrow. His name is Aragel."

"You want to go into Axter? Pray tell, whatever for, young man?" asked Uncle Honza, turning to Aragel, his eyebrows furrowed. Katharina explained that he had come from Arya. It was a good thing Aragel had not shown her his father's journal, though he was tempted to. Katharina was so talkative that she would probably have told Uncle Honza about it, and more people would then demand to see it. Aragel did not feel he could trust anyone with the details of his quest, and he was not sure if they would try anything funny with him.

Aragel backed away as Katharina continued to discuss the Forest of Axter with Uncle Honza; he was still anxious to see more of the cathedral. Her hands were gesticulating and her voice was rising and falling as she spoke, but her uncle remained grim throughout the conversation. It seemed that because of what he had heard, Uncle Honza felt it was too dangerous for Aragel to venture into the Forest of Axter alone, while Katharina felt it was Aragel's business to go if he wanted to, for he was a grown man after all and her uncle should try to help him instead of trying to stop him. It was heartwarming for Aragel to see see her speaking up for him, even though she had barely known him for an hour. It felt as if they had known each other for ages, and it was good to have a friend again.

"Well, let's have him over for dinner then," he heard Uncle Honza say finally from the other end of the cathedral.

"What do you say, Aragel?" Katharina called. "Would you like to come to our house for dinner?" Aragel smiled and nodded. Dinner in a home, a home with a family, sounded wonderful. Relief washed over him as he walked over to join them. He could do with a home-cooked meal again.

***

"Have some more, Aragel, you must be so hungry. All those days out in the forest must have left you so tired," said Ana, Katharina's mother.

"You will stay here tonight with us," declared Uncle

Honza, biting into a corn cob. "It's late and you won't find a safer place to stay." Aragel smiled in gratitude.

Katharina explained that she lived with her family and Uncle Honza's family in a house about two miles from the cathedral. Her family were the keepers of the cathedral and took special care to ensure things there went smoothly and people there were kept safe. It was the only place, as he would find out over dinner, that had remained untouched by the destruction that had overcome Malur. Many houses had been wiped out when, as Katharina put it, "the bad things started to happen", and some homeless people were allowed to stay in the cathedral grounds, which explained the tents. Some of the people who stayed there helped in the cathedral itself, keeping it clean and safe, while others had little shops or other businesses elsewhere in the city. They worked together to provide food for one another, and everyone did their part in making living in the cathedral grounds pleasant.

"Have you thought about how you're going to make it to Axter, boy?" asked Katharina's father, Josef.

"Well, yeah kind of. I think I know the way there from here. I just happened to take a detour to the city when I saw it from a distance." Although he had not intended to, Aragel went on to explain why he had left Arya. He told them about the dark clouds that had loomed over the village for weeks, terrifying everyone.

He told them about Erien and Jaan and why he had made the decision to leave Erien behind. The only detail he left out was that he had been guided up to now by his father's journal.

As he finished talking, he was suddenly aware that everyone was staring at him with deep concentration, as though his story was the most interesting thing they had ever heard.

"You're a brave young man, son," said Josef. "We remember when we first started seeing those clouds. We thought it was just a storm brewing, so we readied ourselves for it. It was only when our crops began to wither and our livestock started to die without any sign of illness that we started to realise that this was more than just a storm. The people of Malur started to get anxious and we did whatever we could to prepare ourselves for whatever it was that was coming."

"Everyone thought it was some sort of natural disaster," Uncle Honza continued. "No one expected the knights to invade our city."

"Knights?" asked Aragel, looking from Uncle Honza to Josef.

"That's right. Knights from other villages decided they wanted to invade Malur. It was most peculiar, since these people often came to visit the cathedral. We tried to fight them off. We built fires around the city, even sacrificing some homes and land to prevent them from coming in. But they were many and their forces were too great for us to hold off. They battered our beautiful city to the ground and took with them whatever they thought was of value. I overheard some of these knights talking one night when I wandered out to gather some firewood. They spoke of the Raggotah and its powers. One of them broke down, saying he felt terrible for doing such horrible things to the people of Malur, but the another said they had no choice, for if they didn't, the Raggotah would kill them."

"The Raggotah?" mumbled Aragel.

"We had heard rumours about this Raggotah," said Katharina. "No one knows what or who it is, but people who speak of it often seem traumatized. I've heard that it destroys life and everything around it with its mere presence. Those who do not die become angry and filled with hate and greed."

"People started doing strange things after the knights left us," said Josef. "Malur was a city of peace, where everyone helped everyone else, and it was a beautiful place to live in. But when the knights had been, things started to change. Even the air we breathed was different; it was heavier and more dense, like trying to breathe through a damp cloth. People started becoming selfish and only doing things for themselves. No one shared anything any more, and those who had less than others started stealing from them. Our livestock had all died one by one and we lost all our trees in the fire we built the night we tried to defend Malur. Somehow anyone who ventured out of the city never came back, so no one dared to go out to gather wood. We ended up having to use whatever we could as fuel for our fires to keep us warm on cold nights. The smell of burning left many of us sick for days, thinking of what had happened here."

"What about Axter? Why does everyone seem to fear the Forest so much?" asked Aragel. Silence fell around the room.

"It's just too dangerous," said Ana. "You're just a young man, you have so much ahead of you, why do you want to venture into something that could cost you your life?"

"All I ever hear from people are these stories about how dangerous it is," Aragel said, a hint of rebellion in his voice. "But I've also heard about the Forest Nymphs that live within the Forest of Axter. I seek them to help Arya – maybe they could help Malur too."

"Forest Nymphs?" questioned Uncle Honza.

"Yes, haven't you heard of them? I was told that they were pure beings and with everything that's been going on, it seems they may be the only things that can help us. No one knows anything about this Raggotah, no one knows what lies within the Forest of Axter. All everyone knows is that some kind of evil is upon us and anything that ventures out of its own home is dangerous. Maybe when the missing people went out there, they didn't have a plan or a guide. But I have a plan. I plan to seek the help of these Forest creatures and get rid of whatever's been plaguing our land all this time."

"I still think it's a bad idea," said Uncle Honza. "You're young and brave, I understand that. But there are some things greater than you, dear boy. Speak to him, Katharina. I'm going to bed." He stood up, clearing his plate. Everyone else joined in to help and by the time everyone was done, only Aragel and Katharina were left sitting at the table sipping on some hot chocolate.

"What? What are you looking at?" Aragel asked. Katharina had been staring at him with an amused smile on her ruby lips.

"Nothing," she replied, taking a sip of her hot drink. But it wasn't a nothing stare, it was a something stare, and if she didn't want to say what it was she was staring about then she shouldn't do it.

"Well I'm glad 'nothing' amuses you so much."

"Who cuts your hair for you?" she suddenly asked.

"I knew it, I knew you were staring. What is it with you and my hair?" Aragel replied.

"It's just different from everyone else's. It gives you

a different sort of personality. Does your wife cut it for you?"

"Don't be silly, I'm not married," Aragel replied.

Katharina's eyes twinkled. "Well you can't have cut it yourself," she said playfully.

"Well I did." Aragel flicked back his hair with a dramatic toss of his head.

"Liar!" Katharina laughed. She was wondering how she was going to persuade Aragel to stay.

Aabel, the leader of the Malur knights, had got wind of the new guest in Malur and his ill-advised quest to visit the Forest of Axter. He had come to the house at dusk just before dinner and spoken to Katharina secretly while everyone was busy preparing dinner.

"Make him stay, Katharina," he said. "Axter is a dangerous place. He must not go. If you want him to stay alive, you have to persuade him to stay."

"But I barely know him, Aabel, how do you expect me to do that? What makes you think he'll listen to me?" Katharina argued.

"Oh, I think he'll listen to you," Aabel replied, smiling cheekily. Katharina's rosy cheeks turned two shades brighter as she smiled and looked away. "Why is he so important to you anyway?" she asked. Much as she liked Aragel, she did not understand the excitement that seemed to surround him and his quest for Axter.

"He is a guest in our city, and as leader of the Malur knights, it is my duty to protect our guests," Aabel replied.

Katharina did not quite believe him. It seemed very strange that Aabel would come all the way to ask this of her, especially as he did not even know Aragel. But she trusted him and promised to try her best.

"Why do you want to go to Axter?" Katharina suddenly asked Aragel, breaking the silence that had grown thick between them.

"I already told you. Do you not believe me?" Aragel replied.

"No, no, I believe you," Katharina said calmly.

"Then why keep asking?" Aragel sighed. "It's getting late and I have a long journey ahead of me tomorrow. I'm going to bed. Goodnight." He put his mug down and climbed to his feet, leaving Katharina alone at the dinner table with her thoughts.

* * *

The next morning, Aragel woke with a start. Suddenly disoriented after a deep sleep, he felt a little scared. Then he recalled everything from the day before, and calmed down, sinking back into the bed and closing his eyes.

"Aragel?" Katharina's voice rang in his ears. He

opened his eyes and saw Katharina's beautiful face looking at him kindly.

"Breakfast is ready" she smiled. "Come and join us. My father has something he wants to tell you."

Aragel got out of bed and washed, wondering what news Josef had for him. The breakfast table was laden with with food; wholegrain bread, butter, jam, fried eggs, fried potatoes, cream, hot chocolate, coffee and tea. Katharina's family were digging in with wonderful enthusiasm. Aragel smiled at their vigour for life and took a seat next to Katharina.

"So, Aragel, my boy!" said Josef, "Did you sleep well?"

"I did, sir. It was the best sleep I've had in a long time. Thank you."

"You're welcome here any time, son. Now, I know you wanted to leave for Axter today, but I'd like to invite you to stay a little longer. You need the rest and I could help you. There's a lot more you need to know before you go on this journey."

Aragel nodded and chewed slowly on his bread, thinking. The sooner he left, the sooner he would find Axter. But then again, Josef was right; there was a lot that Aragel did not know and it might do him good to learn more about the paths to Axter before he made his journey.

Swallowing his bread, Aragel smiled.

"That would be wonderful, sir, thank you," he said.

"Splendid! A wise decision," said Josef. Out of the corner of his eye, Aragel saw Katharina smile as she spread butter on some bread.

"So what's the route you're planning to take?" Josef asked.

"I was planning to explore the caves north of Malur today, to see if I can find a way through them. I'm not sure about crossing through the cemetery though," said Aragel.

"The caves? Those caves have quite a story behind them," said Josef. "They are the resting place of the King of Souls."

"Skeleton? As in bones?" asked Aragel.

Joself shrugged.

"The Skeleton used to be the keeper of Malur, our protector if you'd like. Legend has it that on the midnight hour on the day of the red moon, he lay down in the forest and his body disappeared into the moss, leaving behind only his bones – the Skeleton. People say there was some spell placed upon him and this was his curse. He wandered the mountains and valleys and one day he came across the cemetery that lies before the caves you speak of. He asked the leader of Malur back then if he could use the souls of the dead to keep himself alive and he would in turn lend protection to the people of Malur. Our leader agreed and a deal was struck."

"What happened when he had used up all the souls there?" asked Aragel.

"He would take them from those who were dying," said Josef.

"Isn't that murder?"

"Not if people give them up willingly. People held high regard for the King of Souls and would sometimes offer their souls up to him when they knew it was time for them to go and they no longer wanted to suffer. They would tell their loved ones of their wish and they would then beckon the King of Souls to come and gently draw the soul out of them as they died. It wasn't a painful process for the person dying, in fact, it almost seemed like a prayerful process. The Skeleton respected the bodies from which he was about to consume souls and would thank them for enabling him to continue to live."

"And their bodies? Would they also be buried in the cemetery in front of the caves?"

"Yes."

"How did the knights end up invading the city if there was a protector?" Aragel asked, recalling the stories from the night before.

"Ah yes, you were listening," said Josef, taking another bite out of his bread. "The Skeleton disappeared a long time ago and no one really knows what happened to him. But his cave still holds a trace of his spirit. I do not quite understand this myself, but the legend continues to say that the cave is a death wish and whoever walks into it will have their soul stolen and trapped in one of the many urnes the Skeleton had left behind to keep souls for when he needed them."

"Wow, it's too early in the morning for legends, don't you think Pa?" said Katharina.

"It's never too early for legends! They are after all just fairytales for adults, aren't they?" said Josef, winking at Aragel. Aragel could not be sure, but it somehow felt as if Josef himself did not quite believe in the legends. It almost seemed as if he was encouraging Aragel to go ahead and explore through the caves.

"The caves are actually a shorter route through to Axter," Uncle Honza added. "It's been so many years since the legend has been told, who knows what could have changed. Besides, walking around the mountain instead of going through it would take many days."

* * *

Aragel spent the rest of the day with Katharina exploring the city. She took him to the best stores, and in one of them he met the most curious blacksmith he had ever seen. A jolly old man with rosy cheeks, he hardly seemed like the sort of person one would find amidst all the grey dust in gloomy Malur. They chatted like old friends about weapons, like schoolboys comparing toys. The smith took to Aragel so much that he gave him a club made of ebon wood with a strong silver tip.

Aragel was thoroughly enjoying his time in the city. In moments when he did not think about Axter, he was relaxed, fun, even flirtatious with Katharina. He enjoyed her company greatly and loved her enthusiastic take on life. He wanted more time with her, for he missed the company of another person greatly, and he was not alone there. Katharina enjoyed his companionship too, and in the brief moments when she saw him let his guard down, her heart softened further toward him. Like him, she missed the presence of someone special in her life and it felt good to have someone to share her thoughts with. She found herself opening up to Aragel more than she had with anyone she had ever met, and it was liberating. But Axter never strayed far from either of their minds, and in the little moments of silence that peppered their days together, it was obvious that they both dreaded the thought of the moment when it was time for the parting of the ways.

As the last day turned into dusk and then night,

Aragel and Katharina said their simple goodbyes. After a shy exchange and a warm embrace, they retired to their rooms for the night. Aragel tossed and turned for some time, and finally fell asleep just four hours before dawn.

In the morning when it was time to leave, Katharina and her family bade Aragel goodbye at their doorstep. Ana had prepared enough food to last him at least a week and Josef cloaked him in a leather jacket he had once worn when he had been a young hunter. From her wrist, Katharina undid a copper bracelet that she had carved herself and fastened it around Aragel's wrist. With well wishes, warm embraces and teary farewells, Aragel said goodbye to the family he had drawn so close to over the few days that had passed since his arrival in Malur.

CHAPTER 11

Journey Through
the Caves

Aragel stood staring at the mouth of one of the giant caves. They looked massive and repellent, like the putrid mouths of a horde of cannibals. Tombstones were scattered all around, and the thin air was wet and misty from the rushing river below. The wind pinched his cheeks as it blew across his face, filling his nostrils with the smell of fresh grass tainted by the stink of decomposing flesh. It nauseated him.

He peered into the largest cave, but there was

nothing to be seen, just a stark blackness that stared back at him. Little pathways snaked through the cemetery and naked, dead trees stood leafless amongst the tombstones. Although it was daylight, the only light that seemed to illuminate the place was from strange lanterns that looked curiously like human skulls and cast an orange glow into the misty and dark surroundings.

The cannibal mouth beckoned Aragel into its recesses and as Aragel stepped into it, the stench that met him was so overwhelming that he almost backed out. But instead of stepping back, he stumbled forward – almost as if something had pushed him. He squinted, trying to persuade his eyes to get accustomed to the darkness quicker.

When they finally let him see into the gloom, Aragel saw before him a part of the legend Josef had spoken about come to life. Rows and rows of bottles and urns stood upon shelves carved into the rock walls. Aragel barely noticed the deafening silence in his ears as he walked around, glancing over every urn and bottle that stood against the cave walls.

He walked for about twenty metres before stopping at one particular urn, a white and blue one that somehow seemed different from the rest. Aragel looked at it intently, wondering if it contained a real soul.

Then suddenly the urn, almost as if it had heard

Aragel's question, began to tremble. Startled, Aragel jerked his head back. Then, remembering that the souls could not really hurt him, he regained his composure and picked up the urn. He inspected it for a short while and with steady hands, lifted the lid from it. A puff of dust wafted out, but there was nothing inside it. He set the urn back onto the shelf and waited, almost willing the soul, if there was one, to reveal itself.

He did not have to wait long. A plume of grey smoke began to waft out of the urn. It had no form, no features; it was just a thick grey substance which floated up and mysteriously disappeared into the air. Uncertain what to make of it, Aragel continued walking. As he passed the shelves of urns, he noticed that some of them had been broken.

He realised that he could feel his heart pounding in his ears. It was so quiet that he could hear every rustle of his clothing. It was still almost pitch black, with broken old-fashioned lanterns hanging from the walls. A huge candle chandelier made of wood and metal, now rotten and rusty, lay in the middle of the walkway. An assortment of metal candle holders, stained with the remains of the candles they had once held, projected from the walls. Some still contained candles with their wicks intact, and these Aragel gathered and put in his backpack, using one candle at a time to light his path. Though Aragel's footsteps were like those of elves, soft and padded, he still feared any noise would disturb the peace of the caves.

After walking for some time he came across a room which was bigger than anything he had seen so far in the cave. It had thousands of urns and bottles stacked from floor to ceiling against the walls. The urns seemed different in this room, a little more lively, sensitive, spirited. They rattled as Aragel walked past them and settled down again the moment he passed them by.

Getting more and more anxious that he would get discovered, Aragel picked up his pace. Then, realising that the faster he moved the louder the urns rattled, he changed his mind and slowed his pace. He wondered if the souls within the urns had felt his presence and somehow were seeking his help to let them out.

He looked around nervously to see if there was anyone around, but there was no one. He dropped his shoulders to relax, realising how tense he had been, but the urns in front of him continued to rattle gently on the shelves, threatening to break open, which prompted Aragel to keep moving. He could not afford any unwanted attention, at least not right now.

Images of what might have happened in Malur flashed across Aragel's mind like a movie. He imagined what it might have been like before it had been reduced to ashes – cobbled pathways that lined the streets, with quaint brightly-coloured shop-houses selling fresh bread and groceries with the most succulent fruit anyone ever tasted. Fountains in the middle of every cluster of red-roofed homes, and snow-peaked mountains against majestic skies that gave the perfect backdrop. All this before the knights had invaded and taken away everything from the people of Malur. Aragel saw in his mind's eye the destruction and terror that had gripped the city, taking away everything that was once beautiful and replacing it with gore and grime. He thought about the stories Josef had told him and saw for himself the truth that lay behind it. Whether the King of Souls existed or not, these urns bore within them souls from real people, and someone must have put them there.

Carried away by his thoughts, Aragel hardly noticed how long he had been walking until he felt his knees beginning to buckle. A chamber to his left looked like a comfortable and safe enough place to rest for a while. He placed his bags down on the ground and looked around the room for any signs of danger; there were none except for a few urns lying in the corners of the room. He picked them up and laid them on the ground in a line. Sitting down on the cold ground, he felt the weight of the day roll off his feet. Keeping silent was hard work. His back ached from carrying around his bag and he considered leaving some things behind to lighten his load. He would deal with it in the morning when there was more light. There were more interesting things to deal with now, he thought to himself, his eyes falling upon the urns lined up in front of him. He picked up one urn, inspecting it, rotating it slowly in his hands and taking caution not to topple its lid. *What are you?* Aragel asked silently.

The urn vibrated slightly, startling him. It was as if it had sensed his unspoken question.

"If I let you out, will you talk to me? Can you talk?" He asked in a whisper, afraid to disturb the silence. But the urn remained still in his hands. He placed it back down onto the ground and picked up the next. He asked this one the same question and this time the intricately-patterned urn shook in his hand. He was not sure what it meant, but he at least knew that whatever was inside could hear him.

The candle went out and Aragel lit another, his sixth. Picking up the urn again, Aragel asked, "Would you tell me the story of Malur if I let you out?"

This time the urn shook harder. No longer able to withstand the suspense, Aragel gently took the lid off. A tongue of bluish-white smoke drifted out of the urn, touching Aragel's finger on its way up. It was freezing cold, and it stung Aragel's finger. He whipped his hand away, sending the urn to the ground with a crash that echoed all around the caves. He half expected the soul to fall back down, but it did not. It continued floating upwards, disappearing into the cold darkness of the cave. Aragel stared after it, realising that he would not get anything out of the souls, for they could not speak as he had hoped they would.

Pain throbbed in the finger that the soul had grazed. He looked at it and to his horror found that it had turned black. It felt like it was on fire. He timidly touched the finger and found that there was no sensation in it. Did that mean the soul was evil? Was it a woman or a man, a child or an adult? What had it looked like as a human, and how had he or she died? Then again, the answers to these questions would mean nothing to Aragel. It was late and he was getting too comfortable sitting down. Best to find another place to sleep tonight, he thought, picking up his bag and walking on in the still blackness.

He walked until he came across another chamber that was smaller than the first but looked safe and dry enough for him to seek refuge for the night. He laid out his sleeping mat and sank onto it. The cold ground offered some relief to his sore muscles as he lay down. The entire weight of the day seemed to seep from his body into the ground, and his eyelids grew heavy. He could no longer keep his eyes open. Thoughts of whether the King of Souls was good or evil or whether the souls had meant to help him or not seemed of little importance compared to getting some rest. The sound of silence humming steadily against his eardrums, Aragel closed his eyes and succumbed to the night.

* * *

The next day Aragel awoke to silence again. Leaving behind some old clothes that only added weight to his bag, he packed his things and made his way carefully out of the cave. He found it interesting to see that there were no more urns lining the rest of the way, no obstacles or distractions to prevent him finding the end of the cave. The sunlight felt warm on his skin after a day and a night in a cold damp cave, and he welcomed it with a smile, drawing a deep breath and filling his lungs with cold, fresh air. Autumn had arrived, the greens slowly starting to change to yellows, oranges and reds, and the wind was more brisk and crisp than Aragel remembered it when he had first started his journey.

Standing atop a cliff gave Aragel the perfect bird's eye view. He could see the depths of the valley, where a large village with its streets and rooftops lay surrounded by smaller neighbouring villages. Huge boulders spread all across the valley, and though the dark clouds cast a shadow over the villages, the bright colours of autumn were not to be dulled. Yet there seemed to be no sign of life in the valley, no sign of people, of smoke coming out of chimneys or even beasts grazing in the fields nearby.

From just behind the mountains, a clear river snaked its way down the middle of the valley. Aragel looked past the mist, and not too far away he saw a mountain range that looked different from any he had seen before. The peaks were a soft cyan blue and shiny black. He recognised them from the detailed descriptions and drawings he had seen in the books he had found in his father's room. The harder he looked, the surer he became. These glossy black and blue summits were unique to the Crystal Mountains. They were covered with snow, and a thin layer of mist surrounded the mountains like a cloudy halo. He scanned them and noticed that there were no trees, only huge black and blue crystals shaped like boulders and looking like black and blue pearls in a sea of mountains and snow.

It was a spectacular view, and Aragel decided to rest and have something to eat while deciding which direction he should take next. He hung his legs over the edge of the cliff and pulled out the tomato herb bread Katharina's mother had prepared for him.

Katharina... he wondered how she was. His mind drifted back to Malur and its people as he ate thoughtfully. He missed Katharina and her enthusiastic family and wondered what she might have been like as a child – had she had a best friend? Had they played hide and seek in the courtyards and picked flowers by the rivers nearby? Was she a spoiled child, and had she had many suitors as a young woman? Would he have had a chance with her if he hadn't left Malur?

Aragel stopped himself quickly with the last thought and shifted his mind to Arya; it was too late for regrets now. He thought about his mother and felt a twinge of guilt for leaving her. He hoped Erien had made it back to Arya and Jaan was well with Adomah. Maybe the villagers of Arya in their despair no longer stopped Jaan from leaving, for they now had greater things to worry about. He wished he could have been there for Virto's wedding and imagined the bright happy faces of everyone as they celebrated their matrimony. He imagined everyone seated together at a big dinner table and eating food cooked by Cyrella, as they laughed and listened to Roley's endless stories. He imagined everyone happy and smiled to himself, making himself content with the homemade bread. He missed them all much more than he could bear. It was best to just be thankful for what he had at that time.

Aragel finished his bread and made his way down the steep pathway toward the first village he had seen.

***

Aragel did not know it, but matters in Arya were not at all as he hoped. The people were eating much less than they were used to each day in order to save food, and many were starving. The crops had just been harvested, and they had ample stock to last them a long time if they rationed it carefully. The cold autumn weather was dipping to freezing point in the night, but they could store food deep underground where the ice had not yet reached and the earth was soft. While Aragel sat on a cliff miles away thinking of his mother, Cyrella went about her daily routine in the kitchen back in Arya and thought about her son and what he might have been doing. At least she knew he was safe; Erien had told her everything that happened, and though she did not understand why Aragel had left without him, she knew her son was sensible and never did anything without good reason.

Arya had met with many tragedies, and Cyrella sometimes thought it just as well that Aragel was not around to see the despair that had now overwhelmed the people. It was best that he remembered it as a beautiful place, not this grey dungeon, she'd often tell

Erien, who still felt a little sore over his best friend leaving him behind. The old man who lived next to Aragel and Cyrella had recently passed away and Cyrella knew he would be devastated to hear it. Aragel used to cut the grass in his backyard for a small sum, which he saved up to eventually buy his first pair of leather shoes and overcoat. She recalled how Aragel used to help her and their neighbours run errands, running to the shops and returning at the speed of lightning with everything that was asked of him. She saw his face and the smile he wore when he was presented with the responsibility of running an errand. Then, suddenly overcome with worry over what might have happened to her son, Cyrella forced herself to concentrate on peeling the potatoes for dinner. It would not help her to keep pondering over things she did not have the answers to. At least not right now, when help was needed all over Arya.

CHAPTER 12

Firewood and Friendship

Winding stony paths and dry grassy slopes led Aragel on his way to the village he had seen, the biggest in the valley. He began to meet people, and he asked each one if they needed help with their labour. He thought that if he offered his help, someone would offer him a place to stay in return. But no one needed his help. Everyone in this village seemed to be able-bodied and healthy. He found it curious that there were so many more people than he had expected, since he had not seen a single soul earlier when he was standing on the cliff looking down.

He continued walking and came across an elderly woman carrying bundles of birch branches on her back. Her brow was furrowed and her back bent forward from the weight of the wood. Her white hair peeking out from under a black bonnet that kept it neatly in place. Aragel ran up to her and introduced himself, offering his strong shoulders to carry her burden. She looked at him questioningly with wise brown eyes, uncertain if she should allow this man to carry her load. Sure, it would bring relief to her aching shoulders, but he was a stranger nonetheless. Seeing her expression, Aragel quickly explained that he did not expect anything in return and only sought to help her, since she seemed to be going in the same direction as he was. The old lady considered him for a while and placed the bundles of birch wood on the ground, her expression soft and grateful. They walked in silence with her leading the way. She never allowed Aragel to walk behind her, always making sure she was walking beside him and occasionally gesturing him in the right direction with her wrinkled hands.

After walking for almost an hour they came to a little field with three huts, two standing together and one on its own, separated from the others by a small pathway of grass. The huts looked much too small to be houses, so Aragel guessed they must all belong to the woman. He looked at her and she gestured for him to put down the birch wood. Aragel winced as he unloaded the bundles off his shoulders.

Mirya looked at him quietly for a while and finally spoke. "My name is Mirya," she said. "Come with me." She led him into the hut that stood alone. A small carpet welcomed Aragel into the hut. It was dim, but there were unlit oil lamps standing on the windowsills, waiting to offer light if needed. A stove stood in the farthest corner and in the corner beside it was a small fireplace with firewood stacked neatly next to it. A small round table with three chairs was the centrepiece of the room. Aragel wondered where Mirya slept for the night.

"This is just the kitchen," said Mirya, answering Aragel's question. "The other two opposite belong to me as well. I store wood in one of them and rest in the other. Come have a drink, that was a heavy load you helped me with. Thank you."

Aragel sipped quietly on the cool water and wondered how to ask if he could seek shelter at Mirya's home for the night.

"Are you any good at chopping wood?" Mirya asked quite unexpectedly.

"Yes I am, ma'am. I used to work in the farm back in my village," said Aragel.

"Good. Would you like to help me chop the wood and store it?" she asked. "My arms are tired and stiff in the cold weather and I could use an able-bodied man like yourself to help me." Before Aragel could ask her anything, she added, "You can rest here if you like. You can sleep in this room, if you don't mind. It's small and I use it as a kitchen, but it's clean and the fireplace will keep you warm." She smiled at last. Aragel nodded in acceptance of her offer. Mirya put him to work almost immediately. "Need to start soon before night falls," she said.

She led Aragel to the shed, which was packed with wood, and Aragel withheld the urge to ask how she had managed to get it all in. Too soon for questions, he thought to himself. He worked through the afternoon and evening, chopping as much wood as he could, stopping only for an hour when Mirya prepared him some food for lunch. They ate together in the kitchen and chatted easily over a simple lunch of fried beans and potatoes. Aragel learned that the village he was in was called Balwan and the weather here was generally cold and gloomy with little sunshine. Lately, it seemed there were dark clouds looming over the village, but no one really thought much about them since Balwan was sunless most of the time anyway.

Up close, Aragel could see Mirya's wrinkles and saw that her warm brown eyes were deep set and sunken, as though she had not slept in days. Her hands were worn and her tired shoulders slouched, yet her clothes were clean and she kept herself well. Somehow she reminded him of his mother, and Aragel wondered if this is what his mother would look like when she was older.

When dusk fell and the sky turned a deeper blue, the moon began its steady rise over the mountains and cliffs that surrounded them. Aragel and Mirya sat in silence in the kitchen with their feet in small tubs of water which Mirya had warmed over the stove.

"So where do you come from, and why are you here Aragel?" she asked, moving her toes in the warm water. Aragel hesitated to reply, uncertain if he should tell the truth. Sensing his uncertainty, Mirya assured him, "You can trust me. Who is this old woman going to tell?"

"I'm from the village of Arya," Aragel started. He decided to tell the truth; he figured he had nothing to lose and Mirya might have some advice to share. "I am on my way to the Forest of Axter to search for forest nymphs that could possibly save my village."

"I appreciate your honesty, Aragel. Forgive my intrusiveness, but I must ask, why did you decide to do all this by yourself?"

Aragel explained what had happened in Arya. After he had finished his tale, Mirya did not say a word. She took a deep breath and removed her feet from the tub. The water had gone tepid. She threw the water out onto the grass and sat back at the table with Aragel.

"Can you keep a secret, Aragel?" Mirya asked.

"Sure."

"Good, because what I'm about to tell you is something I have never told anyone in my life. My father once went out into the Forest of Axter in search of the Forest Nymphs. He went because he believed they had special healing powers and would heal him of any illness imaginable. That was almost sixty years ago. He never returned."

"What happened? Why didn't he come back?" asked Aragel.

"I wish I knew, but I don't. Many times over the years I have tried to reach the Crystal Mountains, but I could never manage to get there. It was too dangerous for me. I simply could not get through. Every time I seemed to get a step further than the last time, I had to turn back. There are many sharp crystals blocking the path which cut my feet, and I did not have the strength to get over all of them. Every year I would go back when spring was about to turn into summer, but always I had to turn back before I could reach the Forest of Axter. I never got to see it, but I did make that journey and I can tell you about it."

"So it was these sharp crystals that stopped you getting through?" asked Aragel.

" The crystals were not the most difficult part. The most difficult part was getting through the bodies." She stopped suddenly.

"The bodies?" Aragel asked, horrified.

Mirya looked as if she was going to be sick, but she forced herself to continue.

"There are dead people on the paths to the Crystal Mountains. Hundreds of them."

"Well, I've been through a cemetery and a cave full of dead people," Aragel boasted, half-jokingly.

"No, you don't understand. This place is the most gruesome thing you will ever see. There are decapitated bodies everywhere. Heads stuck on poles and crows feeding on their eyes. Arms and legs scattered all over the place, heads with their eyes pecked out, staring down at you as you walk. That was just the first time. Every year I went, there seemed to be new bodies. The supply of bodies never seemed to end, and there were always vultures and crows feeding on them. I have no idea where they kept coming from. And if you can get through all of that, you still have to deal with the smell of rot. It's like nothing I have ever smelled before, gut-wrenching and repugnant. I had to spit every time I took a breath. The smell would stay in my nostrils for weeks after I returned home.

"Finally, there are the Riders. The insane, wretched Riders, who sleep in the day and tear through the lands at night. They too smell of rotting flesh, and I've wondered sometimes if they are the walking dead. I've got many scars walking through those paths." She pushed up her sleeves to show Aragel the scars of deep scratches and cuts.

"Wow!" was all Aragel could manage.

"All I've got from my journey was this," he said, showing her his blackened finger.

Mirya's eyes widened. "You got that from the caves, didn't you?" she gasped.

"Yes."

"How long ago was that?" Mirya asked.

"Two days ago."

"Then you've got a little more than a week to go. The curse lasts for thirteen days and for those thirteen days, you are not to touch anything with that finger. Everything you touch with it from now till then will die."

Not quite believing what she was saying, Aragel picked a flower out of the vase on the table and touched it with his deadened finger. Nothing happened. Aragel looked at Mirya, who shrugged.

"You'll see. For now, I want to talk about your journey."

"Why?" asked Aragel.

"Because I see myself in you, and you can make the journey that I never could. I failed, but I was never strong like you. Through you, I will fulfil my dream," she said simply. It was not complicated, and Aragel appreciated her honesty. "But it's getting late and there's more work to be done tomorrow. We'll talk again in the morning." She pushed her chair back and rose to her feet. She walked towards the door and bade Aragel goodnight. "I'll leave the lamp on for you, blow it out before you go to sleep, will you?"

Aragel nodded. Feeling deeply grateful for a place to stay for the night, he laid out his sleeping mat on the warm kitchen floor and blew out the oil lamp. He felt as if he was at home, and it had been a long time since he had felt this way. Getting himself comfortable, Aragel curled himself onto his side and fell asleep easily as the moon climbed to its peak in the dark sky and cast its pale light through the small windows.

* * *

In the morning, Aragel awoke to the sound of Mirya calling his name. "Wake up, Aragel. It's time to start the day. Lots to do today."

Aragel woke and rubbed his eyes. Mirya had set the table with bread, butter, jam and eggs. It was simple and divine.

Aragel was about to wash up when something on the table caught his eye. The pretty white flower he had touched the night before was now blackened and limp. Mirya saw him looking at the flower with a horrified stare and smiled discreetly. Aragel felt Mirya's glance and looked up. She met his eye and winked. "Trust me. I know more than you think," she said.

After a hearty breakfast, Mirya led Aragel down to the middle of Balwan. Aragel had bandaged his deadened finger to prevent himself from killing anything else, and carried for Mirya some baskets she had made from birch wood to sell at the marketplace. The town was bustling with people selling produce, groceries, clothes and other knick-knacks. Villagers dawdled about in the stores and bargained with the shopkeepers for a cheaper price.

Mirya and Aragel wove their way through the crowd and finally found a merchant who would buy birch wood baskets. Mirya struck up a bargain and got a good price for all the baskets she had to sell. It was hard work making those baskets and the kind merchant, knowing Mirya's advancing age, was fair and paid her enough to last her weeks. Mirya was pleased and took Aragel to the different shops to buy food for the week. It seemed she planned to keep Aragel for a while longer, for the amount of food she bought was surely more than an old lady could eat in a week.

When they reached Mirya's home, Aragel saw from a distance a bearded, rough-looking young man in the kitchen hut. He stopped in his tracks and held one arm out in front of Mirya, preventing her from walking any further. A little taken aback, Mirya looked at Aragel and followed the direction of his gaze. She started laughing.

"You're a sweet young man Aragel, but you need not be wary. That man in there is my son, Sivis. He must have just come back from his walk in the mountains. Come, let me introduce you to him."

Sivis reminded Aragel of Erien; he was rough, bearded, tall and well-built. Aragel held out his hand to Sivis, who took it with a firm grip.

"Hey, so Ma's bribed you into doing all the work for her, has she?" he said, his face crinkling into a grin. His eyes were warm like his mother's, but Aragel noticed a spark of wistfulness in them. There was an instant connection between the two men as they exchanged formalities.

After helping Mirya to put everything away, Aragel followed Sivis up to a nearby hill that overlooked the town. It was a peaceful village where people were gracious and kind. Wherever Aragel looked, all he saw were cheery, happy faces. It was nothing like gloomy Malur. Balwan reminded him of Arya back in the day when there were no clouds. The clouds still loomed over everything, but Aragel had got so used to it that he barely noticed them. He sat with Sivis, staring out at the people of Balwan going about their daily routine, looking every now and then at the clouds and thinking about everything he had been through till now.

"So how'd you get here?" Sivis asked Aragel. Sivis listened silently as Aragel told him about Katharina, her family and his meeting with Mirya, recounting his journey, leaving out only the journal and the things he had taken from his father's wooden chest.

"So this Katharina girl, she's your girlfriend?" Sivis asked.

"I've told you my story and that's the only thing you're interested in?" Aragel asked with a laugh.

"Well you're a grown man, you know what you're doing. Who am I to try to tell you what to do or how to do it? You'll figure out a way and if you need help, you'll ask. There's nothing interesting about that now, is there?" Sivis replied, raising one corner of his lip. Aragel laughed.

"No, she isn't my girlfriend," Aragel replied.

"But she could have been?" Sivis pressed.

"I suppose..." Aragel replied, trying hard not to get distracted by his thoughts or the emotions that were now beginning to stir in his chest.

"Nice. You think you'll go back for her?" asked Sivis.

"I doubt it, there're more important things to deal with and who knows where this will take me. I can't be letting how I feel over a girl get in the way of trying to find a solution for this," said Aragel, pointing at the sky.

Sivis sighed. "Strong guy."

"Why would you say that?" asked Aragel. "Do you have a girlfriend?"

"I used to," said Sivis picking at a stone.

"What happened? Girl broke your heart?" asked Aragel.

"Not quite. It was an accident. She slipped while we were climbing mountains and fell to her death."

"Whoa, I'm sorry," said Aragel, looking down, embarrassed.

"Nah, you didn't know," said Sivis casually. "Besides, that was years ago. I'm OK now."

Aragel and Sivis continued chatting till the sun began to tuck itself away behind the mountains on the horizon and the sky turned a deep orange and red. They went back to Sivis's house for dinner, where they continued chatting and laughing over funny stories as if they were long-lost family members.

At night, Mirya and Sivis retired to their hut to rest while Aragel stayed in the kitchen again. This time, he left the oil lamp burning. Somehow he felt more comfortable having a little bit of light shining around him as he surrendered himself to his unconscious mind.

Dreams plagued Aragel's sleep that night, dreams and nightmares intertwining themselves tightly around his mind, causing him to kick about restlessly in his sleep. He unknowingly kicked off his blanket and threw a pillow to his side.

Suddenly he woke up with a start. Standing over him was a tall, menacing shadow.

"Who are you? Where are you from? What are you doing here?" Aragel asked in fear. There was no answer. Aragel asked again, but his questions were met with silence. Then the shadow disappeared abruptly into the darkness of the night.

Aragel awoke trembling with fear, and looked around the kitchen for any signs of someone hiding in the corners. Unable to shake off the feeling that he had had this dream before, he recalled when he had left Erien and was resting in a cave the night before he reached Malur. He remembered how he had seen a shadow but was too tired to try to find out what it was. What was someone trying to tell him? Perhaps the guilt of having left Erien behind was playing tricks on him and his tired mind. He tried to will himself back to sleep but it did not come as easily any more and before he knew it, the sun had begun its morning ascent into the open arms of the vast darkened sky.

Since Aragel had woken up before Mirya and Sivis , he took the liberty of preparing breakfast. He dug potatoes from the garden and found fresh eggs in the chicken coop behind the kitchen hut. He told Mirya and Sivis his plans over breakfast and learned from them the path he should take and what he should avoid. They warned him about the crystals and the dangers of the path to Crystal Mountains, and reminded him that he still had a few more days before the curse on his finger would wear off.

"Remember what I said about the dead ones," Mirya reminded him. "Watch you respect them, despite what you might see. Keep yourself safe and trust no one on this journey. The beauty of the Crystal Mountains is deceptive." She prepared some food for him, as Katharina's mother had, and gave him a light blue crystal, telling him he should keep it on him always for protection. Aragel slipped it into his jacket pocket and hugged Mirya.

"I am eternally grateful for your kindness, dear Mirya," he said. "And Sivis, it was good to finally have a brother to talk to again." He grinned.

"Any time, my brother," said Sivis. "Come back here if you need any help, our house is always open to you."

Sivis and his mother stood on the grass pathway that separated the huts and watched as Aragel disappeared into the horizon.

"That young man is as good as dead," said Sivis, shaking his head. Mirya said nothing as she stared after Aragel with tears in her eyes. She sighed, hoping with all her heart that Aragel would be safe and fulfil his journey.

CHAPTER 13

The Path of Horror

The path to the Crystal Mountains was wide at first, the way flanked by boulders of every size and dry stony ground everywhere. As Aragel walked along on the hard, rocky path, he thought about what Mirya had told him and tried to prepare himself mentally for what might come. Images of Katharina distracted him every now and then. He imagined what she might be like if she were with him and smiled at images of her asking endless questions as she walked along cheerfully.

Heaven knows he could have used some cheer now.

He had gone a fair distance from Balwan and the scene before him had become dreary again. The few trees seemed to be faded and dying, the sky was flat and dull and there seemed to be no wild animals or insects about.

Suddenly Aragel felt a chill run down his spine. The hairs on his neck were standing on end, and he felt his face grow pale. In front of him, about twenty metres away, was a human torso, dismembered and impaled on a pole. It had been raised up to make it obvious to anyone who passed.

Aragel braced himself. He took a deep breath and smelled rotting flesh. He continued walking, and the putrid smell got stronger and stronger. It soon filled his nostrils, his throat and lungs. He choked on it and retched, but he knew he had to keep walking. If he stopped, he might not be able to continue. He needed to keep going, and just hope that he would get used to the smell.

As he walked on, he saw more and more corpses impaled on poles. Some were entire bodies, others were dismembered, halved or mutilated. Raggged crows flew from pole to pole, feeding off the rotting flesh. Though he remembered the stories that Mirya had told him, nothing could have prepared him for the sight that was before him. Never in his life had he seen such gruesome and horrendous things. Who would create such horror? What kind of evil lay within the hearts of these people?

The mist around him made everything seen even more eerie and cryptic. The clouds were remarkably low here, and when Aragel looked up at them, he saw what looked like a miniature whirlwind moving silently along below them. He stopped to look at it. After a while, he noticed that whenever the tornado glided over something, the colour faded from it, like a child running an eraser through a colouring book. Trees were losing their lush green, while the grass was turning yellow and then brown. This ridiculous phenomenon kept Aragel rooted to the ground for a long time.

Aragel walked all day and all night for the first time, reluctant to stop, for he feared these strange, deathly surroundings. He took caution not to get in the way of the quiet tornado as he dodged the poles. In the midst of the forest of poles with their loathsome burdens, Aragel found a lone tree that still had its leaves intact. The tree was still green and healthy and its roots were firmly embedded in the earth. The silent tornado had clearly not reached it yet, and he estimated that he could stay there at least till the sun came up again before the swirling cloud of mist enveloped it. He sat down under the tree. He would continue his journey on towards the Crystal

Mountains in the morning. There was a small town called Leghota just beneath the mountains. Mirya had told him about it and he had seen it described in his grandfather's journal. Maybe there Aragel would find rest and refuge. At least for now, he had the food Mirya prepared for him.

He ate slowly. There was no way he was going to fall asleep. Somehow he had the feeling he was being watched, even though there was no one about. He wondered if the dead were really dead, but dared not allow himself to indulge in that thought. He began a long and lonely vigil, his eyes hardly needing effort to stay open. The stench and horror of the place kept Aragel's mind alert as he tried to imagine what might have happened here. Images played through his mind of a black armoured figure holding power over all that had once lived here and giving out orders to kill villagers. Though Mirya had described the place to him, she had not explained what had happened. Perhaps she did not know, or perhaps it was too gruesome to speak of. Either way, Aragel was not sure if he wanted to know.

***

As soon as the sun pushed its orange head above the horizon, Aragel set off once again. By now he had grown slightly more accustomed to the decaying bodies hanging above him and the crows flying overhead to feed on them. Though fear still lingered in his heart, somehow he knew that whatever evil was here, it was not interested in him. He moved his hand to touch the crystal sitting safely in his breast pocket and felt reassured of his safety. At least it was daylight and travel would be easy.

The farther he walked, the fewer bodies he saw. Almost as if he was walking from a black and white world into one of colour, the surroundings changed from dull greys and browns into greens and yellows. In the distance he saw a tree, taller than the rest. Its branches made the shape of a hand. Aragel had seen his grandfather's drawings in his journal and knew his grandfather had walked the same path he now stood upon, for the angle from which the tree had been drawn in the picture was almost exactly the same as his view of it now. He knew he was not far from Leghota. He wondered if his grandfather too had seen the rotting bodies. Feeling slightly relieved and with a lighter heart, Aragel made his way on towards Leghota and the Crystal Mountains, still distant but gradually growing nearer.

When he finally reached the village it seemed small and whimsical, dwarfed by the mountains beyond. A man in brown cotton garments walked up to Aragel as soon as he entered the main gates.

"Aragel, are you?" he asked.

"Who's asking?" Aragel replied defiantly, struggling to recall if he had seen this man before.

"I am Sarosta, the leader of Leghota. Mirya said you would come and asked me to look for you. She has told me of your travels and your plans and has asked me to help you."

"Oh, pardon my insolence, sir. I did not mean to be rude," said Aragel, bowing his head.

"Think nothing of it son. Come quickly, the sun is about to go down and you do not want to be out here when that happens."

As the dark clouds drew over Leghota, so did its mystery. The people of Leghota were beautiful, like Greek gods and goddesses. The women had soft and beautiful features, dark fluid hair and snow-white skin, while the men had strong features and muscular bodies. Though fine-looking, there was something dark about their expressions and a certain mystery lurked behind their eyes. The people greeted Sarosta kindly as the pair approached, but eyed Aragel cautiously as he walked close behind their leader.

Sarosta led Aragel into a two-storey house built of stone and wood. He undid a huge metal bolt and pushed the heavy wooden door wide open to welcome Aragel into his home. The house smelled of fresh bread, which Sarosta had bought from the village grocer.

"How did you know I would come today?" Aragel suddenly asked, standing by the door. Sarosta turned to look at him.

"I didn't. I have been waiting for you at the gate for two days."

"You waited for two days?"

"Yes. I had given instructions to some of my trusted guards to look for you in case I missed you. Come, sit. Have some bread and stew. I just made it this morning."

Aragel was not sure what to make of his sudden new acquaintance, but he had come so far, and trusting Sarosta was a risk worth taking if he could give him rest for the night. Sarosta pulled out the yellow wooden chair tucked in under the table and gestured for Aragel to sit before walking to the stove and pouring two bowls of vegetable stew.

"How do you know Mirya?" Aragel asked over his bowl of stew. It was delicious, and the heat from the stew warmed him nicely.

"Let's just say she used to come through Leghota on her way to the Crystal Mountains, much like yourself. But she never stayed long. Each time she came, she would stay here with me. She never stayed more than three days."

"Was she your...?"

"No. We just enjoyed each other's company,"

Sarosta replied. "She's a wonderful woman to have around and I would do anything for her." Aragel wondered if Mirya was to Sarosta what she was to him, but he understood that asking more questions would only remind Sarosta of Mirya's absence.

"How was the journey here?" Sarosta asked, changing the subject. "Did you make it OK through the Rotting Fields?"

Aragel put down his spoon, suddenly losing his appetite as the memory of rotting flesh filled his nostrils again. He gulped down the food in his mouth, fighting an urge to regurgitate.

"I have never seen anything like it in my life," he said.

"Sorry, not exactly a dinner topic is it?" Sarosta said sheepishly.

"It's quite all right," said Aragel. "Thank you for the food and for offering me help and a place to stay tonight."

"No problem. Now, we're going to have to talk about this crazy mission you're on. You need to know about the Riders."

"The Riders?"

"Yes. The Dark Riders are people who have turned against humanity. They seek power over everything, and for years, they've been trying to take over our lands. They have now almost succeeded."

"What do they look like?" asked Aragel, listening to Sarosta open-mouthed, as though he was his father telling him a bedtime story.

"They are dark hooded creatures, no longer human, although they still have the bodies of humans. They ride the skeletons of elks, and their leaders ride bears. Years ago, my father, a remarkable hunter, was out in the forest looking for animals to hunt when he was captured, along with our village blacksmith, Tyrell. The blacksmith was one of the best I have ever known, he could make anything you needed and do it faster than anyone else I knew. They were both tortured and drugged with poison to make them forget who they were so that they would become slaves to the Riders. My father, in one of his moments of clarity, realised what had been happening and decided to kill himself before the Riders eventually made him hunt his own people. Tyrell, on the other hand, was determined to escape. He believed that if he too were to die, the Riders would only look for more of our people to enslave."

Aragel looked at him with slight disbelief. "That doesn't really make sense," he said. "If the blacksmith is still a prisoner, how did you get to hear of this?"

Sarosta smiled. "You are perceptive," he said. "I saw it with my own eyes. I had gone in search of my father, who hadn't returned in days, and found the place where the Riders dwelled deep in the forest outside Leghota. I watched them for a few days, wondering how I could rescue my father, but I was too late. I saw how they had tortured them and forced them to work. My father was forced to hunt, and they learned skills from him. Tyrell was made to work, and make weapons day and night. My father had a hammer, a special sharp hammer with special powers which the Riders thankfully have not discovered. They knew it was a powerful weapon and gave it to Tyrell to use and make weapons with. They realised that when he had the hammer he would be more productive, so they let him keep it. If they find out the special powers that hammer holds within it, they will be even more difficult to stop and our villages will be overthrown by them one by one. You've seen what they've done to the bodies."

"The Riders did that?" asked Aragel.

"That's right. That entire place used to be a village. But they were taken over by the Riders and the bodies of those they had killed were offered up to the King of Souls."

"No that can't be. The King of Souls is not evil, I've heard his story. He takes the souls of those who have been buried."

"The King of Souls takes souls from anywhere," said Sarosta bitterly. "As long as they are souls, he doesn't care how they are presented to him. If the Riders choose to put them on poles, the King of Souls is not going to protest. All he wants is the souls."

"Why are you telling me all this?" Aragel asked suddenly.

"Because I want you to help me get back my father's hammer. It is the only thing that is going to save us, or at least protect us until this madness is over."

"And why am I risking my life for you?" said Aragel, suddenly feeling rather cocky.

"Your efforts will be rewarded, my friend," said Sarosta.

"Rewarded? I don't need a reward."

"I will give you this," Sarosta said. He picked up a suit of black armour and lifted it up to show Aragel. It looked far too big for him.

"Why would I need that? Its weight will only slow me down."

"I doubt it," said Sarosta, throwing the armour at Aragel, who to his own surprise caught it with both hands. It felt soft and feather-light, not at all the great weight he had expected.

"It's enchanted and it'll protect anyone who wears it. I'm sure it's something you'd like to have with you on your way to the Crystal Mountains?" Sarosta smiled.

"Why didn't you give this to Mirya? You knew she had been trying to journey there for years."

"Your purpose is far greater than hers. Besides, she would never return here otherwise," he said with a wink.

Aragel smiled a grin of acknowledgement. "OK," he said. "I will go along with your plan to rescue the blacksmith's hammer. What's the plan?""

CHAPTER 14

The Rescue

The next day, having prepared everything Aragel would need for his quest, Sarosta saw him off. He gave him a map and showed him the way into the forest where the Riders dwelt. Following the map, Aragel had not gone far before he found the hiding place of the Riders deep within the woods. He hid behind some trees, watching them, planning and plotting his next move. So far everything was going according to plan.

Then suddenly he felt a blow to the back of his head and fell to the ground. He must have passed out for no more than a few moments, but when he regained consciousness, he saw that he was surrounded by hooded creatures. Aragel recognised them immediately. They were the dreaded Riders, just as Sarosta had described them. They rode on elk skeletons, but there were two whose mounts were great black bears. These were clearly the leaders of the pack.

The Riders wheezed as they breathed, and in the cold morning air, Aragel could see their breath condensing in a light greenish mist. Their breath smelled like rotting flesh. The bears wore muzzles and harnesses designed for horses, while the elks, with their huge antlers like tree branches, needed only saddles for the riders. They were the most frightening thing Aragel had ever seen as they towered over Aragel.

He tried to pull himself up, but one of the bears growled deeply, fixing its gaze on Aragel, a clear warning to stay where he was. His eyes filled with fear and his heart thumping wildly in his chest, Aragel tried desperately to think of a way of escape. He could not see the Riders' faces, but as one of them moved in the light he caught a glimpse of its glassy blue eyes and pale, almost translucent, face.

"Who are you and what are you doing here?" said one of the Riders, his voice rasping like nails scratching a board. Aragel flinched.

"I... I... was looking for wood."

"He LIES!" came another rasping voice.

"No, it's true!" protested Aragel, scrambling back as they closed in on him.

"Where are you from?" asked another Rider.

"Arya," said Aragel stupidly, regretting his answer immediately.

"Arya!" the Rider cackled. "Arya, he says he's from, and Leghota is where he comes to collect wood. What do you take us for?" it said, suddenly thrusting a spear at Aragel's throat.

"Don't be impulsive, Thaan!" roared one of the leaders. "He might be useful to us."

With a snort, Thaan lowered his spear. Aragel had no way out. He must either tell the truth and become their slave or be killed. He considered telling them he was visiting a relative in Leghota, but feared the Riders would ransack the village.

Just when he was about to admit that he was going to the Crystal Mountains, a loud crack echoed through the forest. The bears, frightened by the noise, took a few steps back from Aragel, but the Riders pulled on their harnesses, keeping them from running. They looked around, but saw nothing. All of a sudden, an arrow came from nowhere and pierced the torso of one Bear Rider, throwing him off his animal and onto Aragel. Instantly, Aragel felt a cold sensation shoot through his body, shocking him for a second. He tried to move, but was trapped by the weight of the Bear Rider. The cold began to spread through his body, and Aragel screamed in pain. Distracted by the attack, the Riders forgot about Aragel and went into a frenzy, hunting the trees for the mysterious archer.

Just then Aragel saw something move in a tree above them and squinted to try to see clearly. But he was losing his strength, and his vision had become blurred. All he remembered before passing out were gasps and thumps on the ground. Then at last he felt someone lift the terrible weight from his chest.

It was Sivis. He lifted Aragel to safety and unbuttoned his shirt to see the extent of his injuries. "Thank goodness I got to you in time," he said. "We would have lost you otherwise."

But Aragel was barely conscious. Sivis gave instructions to his two companions to scour the area for any other signs of danger while he tended to the young man.

* * *

Two hours passed before Aragel regained full consciousness. By then, dusk was falling and Sivis and his companions had set up their tents for sleeping that night. Aragel could feel a heavy weight on his chest again. He tried to sit up, but felt someone push him back down.

"Rest, my brother," he heard a familiar voice say. "Give it a couple more hours. You're safe now." Aragel opened his eyes and saw Sivis's scruffy face looking back at him.

"Sivis! What are you doing here?" Aragel muttered.

"When you left us, I looked at my mother and said you wouldn't make it alone. She agreed and we both decided it would be a good idea for me to follow you."

"You've been following me this whole time?" asked Aragel.

"Yes," Sivis replied.

"Are you alone?"

"No, I brought three of my closest friends with me Davide, Luca and Nicolai. You can trust them. They're out making sure the area is safe. I'll introduce you to them when they come in later."

"OK. Thank you for saving me," Aragel said, turning his head to look at Sivis.

"We're still in danger. Two Riders escaped and more of them had come out to look for us, but they could not find us."

Aragel frowned anxiously. "Are they still looking for us?"

"Don't worry. They've gone now, but there's no telling how much longer we have. We need to get out of here fast. The Riders are evil and anyone who touches them instantly feels the cold of death. It paralyses the body and makes it difficult to breathe. If the Bear Rider's grip is not released, you can suffocate. Now you need to tell me what the hell you're doing here."

"What happened to me earlier? I felt cold shoot through my body and I was paralysed. It was getting more and more difficult to breathe and I felt my body grow weaker and weaker with each minute," said Aragel, reaching for the water beside him and attempting a sip.

Aragel explained everything Sarosta had told him, while Sivis listened intently. Davide, Luca and Nicolai joined them, all five men agreed that they had to steal the hammer that night or risk dying where they were.

The sky was almost dark now, and they could smell burning firewood in the distance, a sign that the Riders were settling down for the night. Sivis explained that the Riders were communal creatures. They always hunted as a pack, so it was likely that there were no more Riders out in the open for now.

In the dark of the night, Aragel, Sivis and Davide made their way to the Riders' camp, while Luca and Nicolai stayed behind to guard the tents. Aragel walked first, followed closely by Sivis and Davide. The camp, when they reached it, stank of rotting flesh and beer. Bonfires lay scattered about and tents lined up in rows, guarded by the skeletal elks. The elks shook their heads, struggling to stay awake, while the two bears slept soundly outside two bigger tents. Not too far away behind the tents was a small hut, against which spears and bows lay. It was obvious where Tyrell the blacksmith would be.

The three men walked around the circumference of the camp, making their way quietly to the blacksmith's hut. Peering through the window, they saw Tyrell sleeping on his workbench. The hammer lay at his feet, shining in the moonlight. Sivis entered through the open window and clasped a big hand over Tyrell's face to stop him from crying out. The blacksmith struggled and grunted in alarm.

"What... Who..."

"We are your rescuers," said Sivis. "Stay very quiet and come with us. We will not harm you."

Tyrell scrambled to his feet and followed the three men out of the hut, Aragel carrying the hammer. To the relief of all of them, there were no signs that the Riders had been disturbed, and the men were able to escape from the camp with ease.

They returned to the tents to find that Nicolai and Luca had already packed everything. The three men looked at them in puzzlement.

"We need to leave for Leghota tonight," Nikolai

explained. "By daybreak this place will be swarming with Riders looking for us. We have to go now."

"Good thinking. Yes, let's get going straight away," said Sivis.

So the party set off, sharing the load of tents, weapons and backpacks. The journey was uneventful, and they reached Balwan just as dawn was breaking. They made a beeline for Sarosta's home, Aragel leading the way. Sarosta had barely woken when he heard a loud thumping at his door, and answered it to be greeted by six very tired men. Sarosta set about preparing food for the party.

As they ate, Aragel and Sivis related to Sarosta the events of the night. Though Sarosta had been well acquainted with Mirya for years, he had never met her son, and seeing Sivis made him feel closer to her. He welcomed him with open arms. Sivis in turn had often heard stories about Sarosta from his mother, and to finally put a face to her stories made him happy. It was good to see at last this man who had taken care of his mother during her travels.

Though it was the first time everyone had met, there was already a sense of trust between them, as though they had known each other for years.

Later that night, when the evening sun had gone down and their bellies were full from all the beer and fine food Sarosta had prepared in celebration of the rescue of the blacksmith and the return of his father's hammer, Sarosta presented Aragel with the armour as promised. "Put it on, my son," he said.

As Aragel slipped on the armour, he felt it cling to his body as if it was made of silk. It fitted perfectly and did not appear to be too big, even though it had looked enormous before he had put it on. Strangely, as soon as he put it on, he felt a new strength and energy coursing through his veins.

"It will fit whoever wears it and it will protect you well," said Sarosta. "But you must use it wisely and never frivolously, for much as it respects you, you too need to respect it."

That night, when everyone had fallen asleep, Aragel found his way to the top of Sarosta's home and sat on the roof overlooking Leghota. He wondered for a long time if this was going to continue being a lonely journey or if four more companions would now join him. He needed to be sure of what he wanted before continuing. Sure, it would be safer and definitely more interesting travelling with more people, but it would complicate things too. Hiding and getting enough food would be more difficult.

After contemplating this for a long while, he heard the sound of hooves in the distance. He stood up and saw to his horror that a horde of Elk Riders was charging towards the village, bearing blazing torches in their hands. Immediately Aragel clambered up on to the top of the roof and yelled as loudly as he could, trying to warn everyone.

"Riders! Wake up everybody!" he shouted. Then he jumped off the roof and rushed into the house to rouse the occupants and get them to prepare for war. The Riders must have somehow traced them back to Leghota.

A terrible battle broke out in Leghota that night. Houses were set on fire, arrows flew everywhere, and men, women and children were captured and taken as slaves by the Riders. The people of Leghota fought with everything that they had, grabbing hold of home-made weapons, rocks, gardening tools and using fire to defend themselves. But the Riders were too strong. They came to Sarosta's house, smashing doors with brute force, and pieces of debris and dust started floating in the air. Sarosta saw something dark break the wall of dust, coming his way. A heavy, rusty mace with spikes as big as fingers fell onto his left shoulder, throwing him down to the wooden floor. Loud screams rang out as Aragel and Sivis started to fight against two of the riders, but there were nothing they could do to save Sarosta.

They hid in the house for a few moments, peering out at the Riders through the gaps in a wall. Seeing that there was no way they could win this battle, Sivis and Aragel fled Leghota and sought sanctuary in the forest, Aragel with an injured knee and hand. He wondered how bad the injuries would have been had he not been wearing the armour. Sivis escaped with just a few cuts on his back and his hands.

As they hid among the huge boulders that covered the ground, they knew they were still being hunted and the Riders might come back this way when they returned, so after an hour of rest, they continued walking through the forest and down a path that led them to the mountains. At least from here they could see the forest paths beneath them and would know if the Riders were heading their way.

As they sat down in silence, Aragel took Sarosta's hammer from his bag and handed it to Sivis, who took it without a word. Explanations were not needed, for Sivis understood Aragel was trying to protect him. The hammer too had protective powers and since Aragel already had the armour, Sivis could have the hammer.

They spoke solemnly with each other for a long while to decide what they should do next. By daybreak, they had decided that it would be best for Sivis to return to Balwan and use the hammer to make as many weapons as he could to protect Balwan. Since Balwan was not far from Leghota, they were sure the Riders would make their way there next. Sivis would return and prepare the village for conflict. He would train the men, and teach the women and children to protect themselves and show them where they could find safety if need be.

Sivis's village and his mother needed him, so it was with a heavy heart that he bade Aragel farewell and headed back to Balwan. Aragel, deeply saddened and dispirited from everything that had happened, withdrew into himself. He withheld the urge to shout his anger and pain into the wind, for he could not risk being discovered. Swallowing the many emotions he felt arising within him, he picked up his backpack and walked on, towards the Crystal Mountains.

CHAPTER 15

Into the Crystal Mountains

As Aragel walked, he noticed footprints on the ground. Big, deep, five-toed footprints. Wolves!

Aragel remembered his last encounter with wolves and most certainly did not want history repeating itself. He picked up his pace and kept his eyes peeled for any form of shelter where he could seek sanctuary for the night. He walked as fast as he could, ignoring the pain in his knees and the hunger in his stomach.

After a while, in the distance, he spotted a little

hut. Relief washed over him as he walked faster towards it, hoping it would be unoccupied and safe. It was getting dark and wolves were night creatures.

Them out of the corner of his eye, he noticed something move. He turned to look, and stopped in his tracks. A wolf, grey and enormous, stood before him. Its blue eyes were watching Aragel intently, as if warning him not to move. Aragel darted for the hut, his mind racing – should he run or try to fight it off?

Before he could decide, another wolf slunk up and stood next to the first one. Then another, and another one behind Aragel. He was surrounded. There was no way he could fight off four wolves. He was wearing the protective armour, but he was already injured and he did not know if the armour would be any use against a pack of wolves. It was time to run.

Aragel ran as fast as he could for the hut, his heart and mind going faster than his feet could. In a flash, the wolves gave chase and the lead animal pounced. They tumbled together, a ball of human and animal flesh, one fighting for its dinner, the other for his life.

Aragel quickly fumbled for his dagger and stabbed the wolf in the side. Howling in pain, the animal let go, and Aragel ran for the safety of the little brown hut. Darkness shrouded him as he slammed the door shut behind him. Through the small and broken windows, he could see the wolves circling the hut. They were patient creatures and could wait a long time; Aragel knew they were hungry and they had not had their feed for the night yet. Soon, he hoped, they would go in search of some other creature to kill and eat, and that would be his chance to escape.

Looking around at his resting place for the night, Aragel put down his bag and rolled up his breeches to look at his wounds. He felt warmth trickle down his arm and saw that the wound there had deepened as a result of the fall he had taken when the wolf pounced on him. The wound on his leg was no better. He would have to spend the rest of the night nursing his wounds. At least he had some food tucked away in his bag. That would have to be enough for the night. There was no way he would be able to set traps with the wolves pacing outside.

***

"You're crazy, Erien!" Jaan shouted at him. "Who's going to take care of Cyrella? What's going to happen to Arya if you leave? Leave that crazy Aragel alone. He'll know how to take care of himself. You have to stay here and look after Arya!"

Arya's problems had got worse, and Erien was at a loss. Cyrella was falling ill and the entire village was running out of food. Their crops would not grow; no matter how hard they tried, everything was turning brown and grey with death. Even the skin of the Aryan people had turned an ashy grey. Everyone was suffering.

"I cannot stay and watch all of you die, Jaan. How can I stand by, watching everyone suffer? I will only be gone for a few days. Maybe if I help Aragel, things will get better faster."

"A few days! Hah! Look at you and your wishful thinking," snorted Jaan. "Aragel hasn't been back in weeks and you want to find him and be back in days? You're crazy, boy. Stay here and help your people. What are you going to do when you find him? You think this is a hike to the mountains? Look around you, everything is in shambles. What makes you think it is better out there?"

Losing his patience, Erien raised his voice. "If I don't go, we'll never know, will we? I cannot do anything here. We've tried everything to grow the crops. I'm a blacksmith, Jaan, for goodness' sake, not Mother Nature! I can't will crops to grow by singing a song or doing a dance!"

"So what are you going to do when you find Aragel then, hug him and tell him everything that's going on in Arya? And then what? Is he going to come flying back home and fix everything?"

Erien sighed deeply. He knew going to find Aragel

was a long shot, but he also knew it was the last chance for Arya. He figured that maybe if he could find Aragel and join him, things would get better faster. He had to believe that, or he would be as lost and hopeless as the rest of the village.

"I don't know, Jaan. All I know is, going to find Aragel and helping him is better than sitting around feeling helpless. As for Cyrella, she has you and Virto's family. I'm sure you'll all do fine taking care of her."

Realising that there was nothing he could do to stop Erien, Jaan took a deep breath and sighed. "I suppose I can't stop you," he said, relenting to this gentle giant's determination. "What can I do to help you then? When do you plan to leave?"

"I'll go first thing tomorrow morning. While Aunt Cyrella was cleaning Uncle Vaclar's bedroom a few weeks ago, she came across a map, hand-drawn by Aragel's grandfather. It shows the Crystal Mountains and the Forest of Axter. We've figured out a shortcut and if everything goes well, I should be able to catch up with Aragel. He should be at the Crystal Mountains by now. You'll be OK, Jaan. I know you're worried, but it's our only chance. Maybe Aragel needs help too."

Jaan looked out the window stubbornly, smoking his pipe and suddenly feeling very lonely. All this time, Erien had been the one taking care of everyone, a tower of strength for everyone. Now that he was going to leave, what was going to become of Arya? But Jaan himself knew that this was the last chance they had of keeping Arya alive. Erien was right; maybe Aragel did need help.

* * *

Beyond the mist, Aragel could now see the Crystal Mountains more clearly. Rich cyan-blue rocks shaped like long daggers with veins of black running through them covered the flanks of the mountains and glittered faintly above the mist. From where he was standing, he could see thick dark lava oozing between the blue daggers, forming more little daggers as it flowed.

As he entered the valley of the Crystal Mountains, Aragel stood facing the tallest mountain he had ever seen. He looked down at his worn-out boots and moved his aching toes within, wondering if they could withstand the climb.

Suddenly something rustled behind him. Moving his hand swiftly to his dagger, Aragel turned, but saw nothing. He turned back around and just then, he felt a hand on his shoulder.

"Sivis!" Aragel exclaimed. "What the hell are you doing here?"

"I came looking for you. Mother sent me," said Sivis.

"But why? Doesn't she need you to take care of her? You were supposed to take the hammer to your blacksmith and have him make more weapons. What happened to all of that?"

"Calm down. When I got home and told mother everything, she started worrying about you. I thought she would get over it, but I caught her crying one night and when I asked her why, she said she couldn't imagine you going through this whole thing alone. She said she understood the loneliness of this journey too well and asked me to come and look for you. She must have felt sorry for you."

"That's very kind of her, but won't she be lonely? Your house is in the middle of nowhere. What if she needs help?" Aragel was worried about the kind old woman who had helped him so much in his quest.

"She'll be OK. I've told our neighbours to keep an eye on her. She gets along well with them and they're not very far away from us," said Sivis.

Aragel frowned and looked at the ground. He was uncertain about Sivis coming along with him. What if something happened? Who would take care of Mirya? He put his hand on his chest, feeling the armour Sarosta had given him. He would be all right, but Sivis had nothing to protect him.

"You don't seem very happy to see me," Sivis said. He eyed Aragel, trying to read his mind. Aragel broke out of his thoughts.

"No, of course I'm happy. This is not a safe journey Sivis, anything could happen. What if you get injured? I won't be able to lift you. Or worse, what if you die?" said Aragel.

"Oh, is that what you're worried about? Well don't, I've still got this." Sivis pulled out the hammer. "Besides, what makes you think you're any fitter than I am to make this journey?

"Weren't you supposed to leave that with the blacksmith?" Aragel asked.

"I wasn't going to leave it behind with someone I hardly know now, was I? It'll be all right, I told him that we're all in danger and that he needed to make as many weapons as quickly as he could. He's got a few young boys helping him too."

"Well then in that case..."

"To the Crystal Mountains?" Sivis interrupted.

"To the Crystal Mountains," Aragel replied, though he still felt a sense of uncertainty.

As the two men climbed, they exchanged anecdotes about their lives and their dreams, but often they walked in silence. Aragel kept a constant lookout for Sivis. He looked upon him as his brother and trusted him, but something felt strange and Aragel could not stop worrying about it. He made sure that Sivis always walked in front so that Aragel could keep an eye on him.

After climbing for several hours, they found their way barred by a massive archway made of black obsidian stone and black crystals. Above it was a crescent-shaped sign which looked as ominous as the archway. "ENTER TO DIE" it read. Ornaments made of bone hung from every point of the archway and the black crystals glistened threateningly.

"What do you think the person who put that there was trying to tell us?" Sivis asked with a wry smile.

"Well I hope you've fulfilled your last wishes, my friend," replied Aragel.

As they passed under the archway, an overwhelmingly pungent smell of rot engulfed them. Decomposing bodies and dried bones lay everywhere. Smaller broken and ruined versions of the dark archway with more warning signs studded the path in front of Aragel and Sivis. More bodies piled up with each sign they passed, all mutilated, pale and dried out, as if someone had sucked the blood out of them before they had died.

Sivis, unable to take the stench any longer, bent over and vomited. As he did so he was horrified to see the hollow eye sockets of a decapitated head staring back at him. He stumbled backwards into Aragel who was desperately trying his best to keep his own food down. This was worse than anything he had seen.

"This is disgusting," said Sivis, retching again.

"Hold a cloth over your face, it might help," Aragel replied, his voice muffled through his sleeve.

"It smells like there's blood rotting somewhere. Like dead fish... or worse," said Sivis.

"We ought to keep going, we should get used to it after a while," said Aragel.

"I doubt it," Sivis grumbled. "What are we doing here? What are we looking for?"

"I don't know. People? You know, if you talked less, you'd have to breathe less." Aragel was struggling with the stench, but it wasn't the only reason he wanted Sivis to stop talking. He was asking questions that Aragel didn't have the answers for.

The two friends braced themselves and walked in silence through the gloom. Soon they came to a small town. A church surrounded by a few small shrubs stood ruined and abandoned in the centre, while small houses with bone ornaments hanging from their broken roofs stood around. More horrendous smells were issuing from them.

Sivis went towards a small grey hut. As he drew closer, he realised that the entire hut was made of bone, and some parts were covered with rotting flesh.

Aragel walked cautiously into the church. Memories of meeting Katharina in a similar building flashed into his mind. The building appeared empty, but some candles were lit, so it was obvious that there were still people around. A figure moved in the background near the altar and Aragel moved closer to see who it was. As he called out, a pale, shrivelled, grey-skinned man turned to him. His face was sunken and pale, with eyes deep and hollow, and he wore a black robe and no slippers. He stared into Aragel's eyes, but he did not speak and Aragel did not dare ask any questions. Instead he simply nodded and walked silently away.

The men left the building and continued down the road into the town. Just as they were about to give up on their hopes of finding anyone in this town, they began to see more people. They all wore similar robes, torn and grey as if they had not been washed in months. Aragel noticed that their skin was like that of the man they had seen in the church. Everyone seemed to have the same pale, pasty skin, slightly bluish, like that of a dead man. Everyone looked malnourished, and they all had deep hollow eyes that stared after the new foreigners to their town. Skinny stray dogs roamed freely, flies hovering around their wounds, most likely sustained in fighting one another for food. One stray hobbled over to Sivis and sniffed him. It tried to gently bite into his leg, almost as if it did not want to cause him any harm, just to say that it was hungry. Sivis kicked the dog away, but it came at him again, fixated on Sivis's leg, obviously desperate to fill its empty stomach. Sivis feared that the stray had a disease, and he swiftly pulled out his dagger and slashed its throat, killing it instantly.

Instantly there came a blood-curdling scream, and they turned to see a woman howling at them. Like a chain reaction, the woman was joined by two others, then five more, and before they knew it, everyone around them, men, women and children, was screaming at the two men. Grey-faced people in rags with empty eyes screamed at him in a tongue that was foreign to both Aragel and Sivis. There were at least of thirty of them. Then suddenly, as if someone had blown out a candle, everyone went silent and walked off purposefully in different directions. They simply dropped whatever they were doing and walked away. Aragel and Sivis exchanged glances and eyed the deathly-looking people cautiously, afraid that one step might set them off again.

They realised that everyone seemed to be walking back towards the centre of the town. Their movements were calm and focused, and they barely batted an eyelid as they walked. People weaved in and out of one another's paths as the two men stood and stared at this strange phenomenon.

"Look!" said Sivis, pointing. To the northeastern side of the church, bright orange flames were licking the sky some distance away. At first it seemed something had caught fire, but the flames were coming from a high pedestal in a distance and Aragel saw a man standing close by; he looked remarkably like the old man Aragel had seen in the church. Strangely drawn to the sight, the two men walked quickly towards the flames, feeling their faces get hotter as they drew closer. They did not speak or look at one another; their gaze fixed on the flickering orange light, they moved just as the villagers had but quicker.

Neither of them saw the hole in the ground between them and the fire until it was too late. The fall broke both of them out of their hypnotic state and they scrambled to their feet to find themselves in a pit studded with sharp wooden spikes. It might have been a trap for animals, but it seemed too big. If it was for humans, what was it doing here?

Aragel picked himself up. "You OK?" he asked Sivis. It seemed neither of them had been seriously harmed, but both men had scratches on them and they feared some form of infection. They washed their wounds quickly with their precious drinking water and bandaged them with some cotton cloth Sivis had brought along in case of injuries like this.

The two travellers pulled themselves from the pit, taking great care not to suffer any further injuries. As they climbed out and looked around, they realised that the entire place was studded with traps.

"What do you think these are for?" said Sivis, tugging at a rope that was attached to a device that looked like a smaller version of a bear trap. It would kill an unsuspecting victim in an instant with its sharp toothy jaws.

"Animals, maybe?" Aragel replied, furrowing his brows as he looked into another pit.

"Maybe," said Sivis, "But they're too big. And look at this, it's too lightly-built for animals. And why would anyone need so many traps?"

"I think I know why." Aragel's voice trailed off as he stared into one particularly big pit. Sivis walked over to the pit and saw an arm lying in it.

"Oh, that's vile. They can't be cannibals, can they?" asked Sivis, "Eating what they kill?"

"It's a wretched thought, but they might. I've never seen anyone look so undernourished before and people do crazy things when they're hungry. Even eating each other."

The blaze had been reduced to a small fire by the time Aragel and Sivis reached it. The man Aragel had thought he recognised turned out to be a scarecrow which looked suspiciously as if it was made of human parts.

Then, from a little house in the background, the old man from the church emerged. Dressed in respectable blue robes, the old man stepped out through the smoke and mist and stood before the two puzzled men. As he drew closer, they heard him muttering, "Terror, terror is rising, it's a sign, I knew this would happen." He looked grim.

CHAPTER 16

Prisoners

"Sivis!" Aragel whispered, looking around them.

"What?" asked Sivis. Then he saw what was happening. Without either of them realising it, the townspeople, in their hypnotic stupor, had quietly surrounded them. A trap! The bonfire, the screaming, had simply been to get the attention of the two men and bring them to where they now stood.

Aragel's fingers wrapped tightly around his dagger, in case someone tried to attack them. Sivis watched cautiously, holding his hammer firmly in his hand.

"Who are you?" asked the old man.

"We're travellers. We are passing by your town on our way to Axter."

"I didn't ask you where you were going. I asked who you were," the old man replied.

"We've answered you. We are travellers" said Aragel assertively.

"Ah, a wise one. Let's try again. My name is Venor. Who are you?" he asked once more.

The travellers hesitated. The old man frowned, considering the two well-built travellers suspiciously with his dark grey eyes. "I have no time for this!" the old man declared impatiently. "Throw them in the dungeon! Maybe they'll remember who they are there."

The dungeon lay beneath the town and was cold, dark and damp. It smelled of human waste and decomposing bodies. An evil-looking, toothless man watched the gates and smiled cruelly when he saw Aragel and Sivis led by two burly men wearing black hoods. They were pushed into a cell, where two plates of rubbery meat and two tin cups of rusty-looking water sat waiting for them.

"Welcome to our humble inn dear sirs," said the toothless watchman, his voice coarse and dry. "You'll find that in this restaurant we serve fine cuisine prepared by the finest chefs of our town." He let out a cackle as he walked way.

Hungry from not having eaten since morning,

Aragel and Sivis wolfed down the food and drank the rusty water, holding back the urge to throw up every time they swallowed. The cell was cold, with just a few candles for light. On the walls were stains that looked horribly like human waste and blood.

"That was vile," said Aragel after forcing down his last morsel of food.

"I don't know how you even finished it, I couldn't," Sivis said, looking at his own food. "I did not dare to even think what it was."

Aragel shrugged. "I didn't think, I was hungry so I ate. Could we talk about something else please? I feel that taste coming back up just thinking about it."

"What are we going to do now?" Sivis asked.

"I don't know. I don't even know what happened up there. The people are weird. Their skin, the way they behave, it's not normal," said Aragel. "I feel different in this town too. I feel this chill in my bones, and my mind is blurred for some reason."

"Yes, I feel that too. Maybe they've got some sort of magic powers."

"Maybe, but I doubt it. The old man did look like some sorcerer, though sorcery has been unheard of for years," said Aragel, spinning the metal plate on the ground.

"If I was a sorcerer, I would've killed you both instantly." came the solemn voice of Venor beyond the bars, startling Aragel and Sivis into silence. "Patience is not one of my virtues. Now tell me, who are you both and where are you from?"

"Since you've already locked us in here, there's no need for us to tell you any more now, is there?" Sivis shot back. It was plain to see that he wasn't in the mood for jokes, or even to be compliant.

"Well that depends. Your secrecy over who you are makes me doubt you. And I don't like being in doubt. If you find your current living arrangements suited to your liking, then go ahead and keep your identity a secret. Otherwise, you'd be wise to tell me your intentions here." He turned to walk away.

"Wait!" Aragel called out.

"What are you doing?" Sivis whispered harshly.

"Shut up," Aragel said to Sivis. "Wait! Venor!" Aragel's echoed through the empty walkway.

"Aragel, you don't even know this man. What if he is some sorcerer? What if he goes looking for our village to take over? It's too dangerous." Sivis tried to reason.

"Trust me," said Aragel.

"Come around, have you?" Venor had suddenly appeared from nowhere. He stood just outside the cell, peering in between the bars at the two men.

"What the...?" Sivis muttered. Aragel glanced at him and turned to look at Venor. Looking him in the eye, Aragel began to speak with confidence.

"My name is Ludek and he is Zoromir. We're from a village far beyond the Crystal Mountains called Kaliste."

Venor smiled. "You're lying. There is no such place as Kaliste anywhere in this part of the world."

"You're right," replied Aragel. "It is not in the region of the Crystal Mountains and in fact it no longer exists, after a terrible disaster tore the village apart. It has taken us many months of travel to get here, sir." Aragel maintained eye contact with Venor, almost believing what he was saying himself.

"Very well," said Venor and he turned to walk away.

"Wait, you said you'd let us go if we told you!" Sivis yelled.

Venor stopped to turn and said, "I never promised to let you out of your cell. I only said you'd be wise to tell me your intentions. What can I say? You're wise." He smiled and bowed his head slightly. "Goodnight travellers," he said as he walked away into the shadows of the walkway.

"I told you it wasn't worth it," said Sivis.

"Could you shut up, please? We didn't have a choice. And stop talking. He seems to show out of nowhere, it's best we keep silent until morning," said Aragel, looking at Sivis with knowing eyes.

Sivis knew he could trust Aragel, and that he was smart and not one to act rashly. Maybe he was right; it was best to be silent for now, at least till morning. The two men huddled back to back in the freezing cold and willed themselves to sleep in the dirty cell. The smell bothered them no longer.

In the morning Aragel and Sivis woke to the clanking of metal on metal. The watchman was banging a tin cup on the cell bars.

"Wake up, sleepyheads," he said mockingly. "There's work to be done." The two men pulled themselves up, the sudden smell a stark reminder of where they were. "Freshen up your pretty little faces and go up. Master Venor is waiting for you," said the watchman.

At the top of the stairs, the sunlight dazzled their eyes, blinding them momentarily. Master Venor was waiting for them just as the watchman said he would be. A burly looking bald man with a pot belly stood next to him.

"Good morning gentlemen, I trust you had enough rest for the night?" asked Venor with a grin. The two men stayed silent. "We can put those strong young bodies of yours to good use. You will help Boris here with whatever he needs." He patted the shoulder of the burly man. "They're all yours, Boris. Be kind to our new guests," he added, the corner of his mouth turning up slightly.

Aragel and Sivis heard the sarcasm in Venor's voice and knew they were in for anything but kindness. As soon as Venor had left, Boris clouted them both on the backs of their heads and put them to work. They were made to draw rusty water from the well and start clearing the mess in the streets.

As Aragel drew up their fifth bucket of water, he noticed someone crouching over another bucket. He called out to him to go away, but the man did not move. Aragel looked at Sivis, who was closer to the man, and gestured for Sivis to get rid of him. As Sivis did so, the man turned to look at Aragel. Rusty water was dripping from his chin and he looked like a predator feeding off its kill.

Aragel turned to look into the well, and this time he saw a dismembered leg sticking up from the surface. With a shock, he realised that they had been drinking bloody water the entire time. Suddenly feeling sick, he let go of the rope tied to the bucket, allowing it to hit the water with a loud plop.

He walked away and sat under a tree to compose himself. Fifty metres behind him, a small bonfire was burning. People sat around it, roasting meat. Aragel peered at them from behind the huge tree trunk, observing them and wondering why these people needed to drink blood-tainted water. Apart from the incident the night before and the way they looked, these people seemed no different from the people of Malur. There were six of them gathered in a circle around the fire; two were standing, three were sitting and one was lying down. Every now and then, someone would prod at the man on the ground, as if to get him to wake up and join them for a meal.

Aragel was just about to return to Sivis when he saw a woman pick up a huge knife and place it on the arm of the man lying supine on the ground. Then she calmly drove the knife into his abdomen and disembowelled him in front of everyone. There were no screams; the man was clearly already dead. It was his flesh they had been roasting at the fire.

Horrified by what he had just seen, Aragel ran back towards Sivis, who was still pulling buckets of rusty water from the wells.

"What's going on? You look sick," said Sivis.

"I'm not sick. The people here are sick. They're cannibals, Sivis. They eat humans and drink blood mixed in water. Look into the well," Aragel was panting in shock.

Sivis peered in and saw what Aragel had seen. Then he walked to the tree where Aragel had hid and saw the cannibals feasting.

"Oh god, that is disgusting," Sivis mumbled.

"We need to get out of here, tonight," said Aragel.

The two decided that when they returned to their

cell that night they would hatch an escape plan. In the meantime, they had to do as Boris commanded. They spent the rest of the day without food or water, drawing up the bloody water from the well, heaving dead bodies onto a wheelbarrow and discarding them in a ditch close by, and cleaning up the piles of human waste from the street.

They returned to the dungeon that night escorted by Boris and exhausted from the day's work. As Boris handed the two men over to the watchman, Sivis noticed that the watchman's usual aggressive demeanour had softened. He seemed relatively passive tonight, and no longer interested in his new guests. As he led them back to their cell, the watchman muttered curses at Venor, calling him 'unreasonable' amongst other things.

"Bad day today?" Sivis asked, attempting a conversation.

"Shut up," the watchman snapped.

"Can't have been worse than ours," Sivis went on. "Never seen so much dead nor cleaned up so much crap in my life. What do you do, you just sit here and watch the place? It's so tiny, I bet you get to sleep all day."

"Tiny?" the watchman said suddenly. "You think this place is tiny? Look again, you daft fool," he said, waving his torch around. The light revealed long tunnels and many doors. "Try cleaning up this place yourself. At least there's two of you. Now get in and shut up." He pushed them both into their cell and slammed the cell door shut.

"Hey man, if you're pissed off at Venor, don't take it out on us. We've had a hard day too. We didn't even do anything to be here," Aragel replied. The watchman kept silent, but Aragel sensed that he was mellowing. "What did he do to piss you off anyway?"

"I don't want to talk about it. I shouldn't be talking to you," said the watchman, turning to leave.

"Wait! Hang on, what's this in here?" Sivis called out to the watchman.

"You're in a cell. It's probably a wall," came the toothless reply

"I'm not daft, there's a handle here. Look, Aragel, I think it's a door." The watchman stopped in his tracks.

"Can't be," he muttered to himself. "I put them in the doorless cell, didn't I?" He turned back round. "Let me see." He pushed his key through the keyhole and turned it vigorously. Aragel and Sivis exchanged glances. "All right, now…" said the watchman. But before he could finish, Aragel and Sivis pulled him in and hit him on the back of his head with Sivis's hammer. He slumped to the ground unconscious.

"Hurry!" Sivis whispered, "we don't know how long we've got." They ran through the dungeon, looking for a way out. Most of the doors were locked. They were made of solid oak and would be impossible to break through. The doors that were open appeared to lead nowhere. They followed a winding passageway. The deeper they went, the more they feared that they would be trapped with no way out.

CHAPTER 17

Escape from the Crystal City

"Looking for something?" a familiar ominous voice came out of the darkness.

"Damn!" Aragel muttered, casting the burning torch in the direction the voice had come from.

"Were you looking for a way out?" Venor asked casually. The men stayed silent. "Sorry boys, there is no way out. You're actually lucky you bumped into me. A bloke could easily get lost in this maze of a dungeon, you know." He pointed to his left. Aragel shone the torch over to see a skeleton lying slumped against the wall. He took a step back.

"If you don't want to end up like him, my friends, you'll find it in your best interests to return to your cell," Venor said slowly.

Aragel and Sivis turned and started walking back to where they had come from, wondering how they could prevent Venor from seeing the injured watchman on the ground.

"Why do you want us here? What good are we to you?" Sivis asked.

"I asked you for your names and where you were from and you didn't want to tell me. You made me think I can't trust you, and I don't like people I can't trust, so here you are."

"But we've told you who we are and you don't seem too angry that you found us trying to esc…" – Sivis saw that Aragel was glaring at him – "look around," Sivis finished. Venor gave a hollow laugh.

"Why should we bother to get angry and kill you when you clearly enjoy the work we've given you and you're making a good job of it?" said Venor, "I've learned in the last few days that sometimes violence isn't the way to go. Especially when you can find a use for people," he said, stopping at their cell. Aragel looked around. They seemed to have got here a lot more quickly than he had expected. The watchman was on his feet by their cell gate, staring at them with eyes of hate.

"Get in," he growled.

"Now, now, let's not get testy. We treat our guests with kindness here, don't we?" Venor said, his mocking voice almost sickening. Aragel and Sivis walked into their cell to see a decomposing body lying in the middle of it. The smell made them retch immediately.

"Oh, I took the liberty to bring your food to you today boys, I thought maybe you'd enjoy it rare this evening," Venor said calmly. He smiled a sinister smile and turned to walk away, leaving Aragel and Sivis to figure out what they were going to do. Even if they moved the decomposing body, there was no way they were going to lie where it had been. They had to sleep leaning against the dirty cell walls. Not surprisingly neither of them slept well, being constantly awoken by the stench and haunted by the irrational fear of being attacked by a decomposing dead body.

* * *

The next day, Aragel and Sivis awoke to the smell of something burning and realised there was smoke everywhere. The watchman was nowhere to be seen, and they could feel the dungeon get hotter. Panicking, they began shouting for help.

"Shut up!" It was the watchman's voice. "Haven't you seen a little bit of smoke before, ladies?" he mocked.

"What's going on?" Sivis demanded.

"Why don't you go up and see for yourselves? Boris is waiting for you anyway," he said, letting them out of the cell and up through the stairs into the smoky daylight. Not far away from the entrance to the dungeon, a huge bonfire burned. Wheelbarrows loaded with bodies stood next to the fire and people were tossing them into the fire like wood. There was no smell, as Aragel remembered from Malur.

"Enough sightseeing for today. There's work to be done," said Boris from behind them. He led them to the church they had passed the first day. "This needs to be cleaned. The full moon is coming."

"OK, what do you want us to clean?" asked Aragel.

"This," said Boris gesturing at the church.

"This?" Aragel pointed at the church, "this whole thing? You want this whole thing cleaned? Are you insane? There're only two of us."

Boris smiled nastily. "I told you there'd be plenty of work today. I'll be back in a few hours. And don't bother trying to run away. Venor'll know," he said and lumbered away.

Sivis and Aragel set to work. They started by clearing the area of human parts, then went on to sweeping. By the time they had got down to mopping, they were both exhausted. Both agreeing they could not work any more, so they decided to go around to the back of the church, where they would not be seen so easily, to rest. When they got there, they both slumped against the wall and stared at the smoke billowing in the distance.

Then they noticed two scarecrows leaning against the wall looking as if they too had had a long day's work.

"Look at that, he actually has more of these things. I wonder what he uses them for, I doubt if it's to scare away birds," said Aragel.

"Hey Aragel," said Sivis switching his gaze from the smoke to the scarecrows, "I think I have an idea. Come and help me with this. Quickly!"

Aragel stood and walked over to the two scarecrows, which stared back at him with blank eyes. They pulled the scarecrow towards them and started dragging, each one taking one straw-filled arm in his hands.

"Where are we going with this?" asked Aragel.

"Over there," Sivis replied, nodding towards the north east. Aragel realised what Sivis's big plan was. He was going to set the scarecrow on fire.

"Are you sure this is going to work?" Aragel asked, uncertain.

"You saw what happened that evening. There must be something about these strange things and the fire that attracts these weird people," Sivis said, his shoulder bowed under the weight of the scarecrow.

"What about Venor though? He seems to know everything all the time," said Aragel.

"I don't know man, but I do know that this will at least attract the villagers and without the help of his people to throw us around I doubt Venor's got the power to do anything." Sivis seemed uncertain about what he was saying.

"I hope you're right, otherwise it'll be us on a pyre," Aragel replied, heaving the deadweight straw man higher up onto his shoulders.

The two travellers dragged the scarecrow to the same place they had once been attracted to and laid it on the ground. "We need fire," said Aragel, turning back to the church. "Wait here!"

He ran quickly back to the church. There was no time to spare, for Boris would be back at any moment. The thought of the decomposing body in the dungeon cell gave Aragel the extra boost he needed to run faster. When he reached the back of the church, he stopped to catch his breath. He needed to look as normal as possible if he were to bump into anyone here. He walked around the wall towards the side of the church, where he noticed an entrance to the main hall where he had his first encounter with Venor. He spotted an oil lamp burning at the altar and walked slowly towards it.

"What do you think you're doing?" A voice suddenly boomed through the halls. Aragel's heart froze as he turned to see Boris standing at the church entrance.

"We just cleaned the floors and we were going to get started on the walls," he lied, praying silently that Boris was just there to check on them and leave quickly.

"Where's your friend?" Boris asked, looking around.

"He's out at the back," Aragel replied quickly.

"What's he doing there? I want to see both of you."

A sense of calm overcame Aragel's mind at that moment and he replied casually, "Oh, he's um, clearing his bowels. Fourth time he's gone today. Doesn't really take to the food here you see."

"That's disgusting. Make sure he cleans up the mess he makes, or that's what you'll both be sleeping in tonight," said Boris as he turned to walk away.

"Boris!" Aragel called out after him.

"What?" Boris replied, his voice gruff.

"How long do we have to clean up the walls?" Aragel asked. Boris looked at him and frowned.

"I'm just asking because I don't want to disappoint you," Aragel quickly added.

Boris looked around. "You've got till dinner time.

Make sure the entire place is spotless," he growled and walked away.

Aragel waited until he was out of sight before grabbing the oil lamp and making a dash for it. He ran back to Sivis faster than he had run to the church and saw him lying down next to the scarecrow. Fear gripped his heart as he approached.

"Sivis!" He called out. Sivis opened his eyes with a start.

"What took you so long?" he asked, getting up.

"Get up, man! Boris was there! He had come to check on us and I told him you were out back with a stomach ache. He didn't wait for you and left. Said we had till the end of the day to finish cleaning the church."

"Yeah, well that's not going to happen," said Sivis, bending down to lift up the scarecrow. There was a little hole in the ground that fitted the scarecrow's stand perfectly. A shiver ran down Aragel's spine and the hairs behind Sivis's neck stood on end. They knew they were standing on the site of some ritual, and their hearts pounded. Aragel broke the oil lamp at the base of the scarecrow, setting fire to it. The dry straw caught fire quickly and soon enough orange flames danced around the scarecrow, clawing at it with fiery fingers

Aragel and Sivis waited at the scarecrow's side for

a while, listening. At last they heard it; a blood-curdling scream from far away echoed down the wind. The scream became two voices, then many. If everyone from the village was drawn by the blazing scarecrow, they might be able to escape safety through the same terrifying entrance they had entered the city by.

Knowing that they could not be seen, they ran due east away from the church. Here they hid behind some trees and watched as people started rushing towards the building.

"Who set the crow on fire?" Venor yelled at the watchman, pulling him by his shirt.

"I don't know, sir, I've been in here with you the whole time," said the watchman, taken aback by Venor's sudden aggression.

"You don't understand, watchman," Venor growled. "No one is allowed to burn that scarecrow except me." The watchman looked at him in silence. Venor continued, "These scarecrows are different," he said, pulling up his sleeve to reveal that his arm was turning black, as though it was getting burned. The watchman looked at Venor's arm, terror filling his widening eyes.

"Why...?" he started.

"It's a curse," Venor said, anguish in his voice.

"Then why burn them in the first place?" the watchman asked.

"It is my only way to get everyone to listen to me," Venor replied, pulling his sleeve down. "It was the condition the King of Souls placed upon me when I begged him for mercy and asked him to allow me to continue as the city's leader. I've got to go now." He ran out into the sunlight, looking around to see that the city had almost emptied. Everyone was heading towards the fire. Venor ran to a group of them, trying to stop them, but no one took any notice. "Stop! It's me! Your leader is here and he speaks! Stop now!" He screamed ever louder, but he knew in his black heart that the curse of the King of Souls reigned and no one would listen to him. He started to run towards the fire, thinking that if he could douse the flames, his people would wake up and return to him.

Aragel and Sivis saw Venor approaching the church and set off towards the city gates. They should be safe now that they knew where he was. Venor's face was white, and his confidence had evaporated. He was clearly terrified of the giant flames that continued to devour the scarecrow. Then Aragel saw that Venor's hands had turned black. He looked down at his own hand, the one from which he had lost a finger in the Cave of Stolen Souls. He had no time to sit and ponder, for someone would soon realise they were missing.

The two travellers soon broke into a jog and finally began sprinting, back past the church and past the houses they had seen when they had first entered the city. They ran past the dismembered bodies and the signs of death, feeling as though they had a chance of beating death this time. The smell of fresh air hit them like a blessed relief, filling their lungs with the clean oxygen that they had missed for what seemed like an eternity. At last they were out of the city, and safe.

* * *

Back in the city, Venor was growing desperate. "Put out that fire Boris, put it out now!" he commanded. The entire population had now reached the spot and stood blankly before him, staring at him, expecting a command.

"What's going on, Venor, what's wrong with your hands?" Boris demanded, looking at Venor's hands. They were now charred and black.

"It's the curse, Boris," Venor said, averting Boris's gaze.

"What curse?"

"Years ago, when the King of Souls came to our city in search of souls, I promised him a hundred and I promised him that I would take the souls of those who were already dying. We didn't have enough, but it was a promise to the King of Souls in return for protecting our city. I knew the consequences if I did not keep up the end of my deal, so in desperation, I commanded the execution of a hundred people for petty crimes, anything they could be accused of. The King of Souls found out and called me spineless, he said I was as empty as a scarecrow and cursed me, making me the leader of a city of barbaric people living in squalor. Only I can burn these scarecrows Boris, otherwise I will burn myself. You have been my right-hand man for ten years. Help me! Put out the fire please, before I burn any more!"

Boris saw the pain in Venor's eyes and saw him weakening as the fire continued to burn, but his stoic expression did not change. "So you're the reason our city is the way it is?" he said quietly. "You're the reason why we feed off our own, and you're the reason why we have never been able to free ourselves from this squalor?"

"Please Boris, please save me," Venor begged. Boris merely looked at Venor. There was no compassion in his eyes as he stared into Venor's pained face. It was obvious who had started the fire, for Aragel and Sivis were nowhere to be found. That did not matter to Boris, for they served no purpose in the city.

Without a word, he grabbed Venor by his charred hands and without a second thought, pushed him into the fire. Venor's screams seemed to echo across the Crystal Mountains as the flames claimed him as their own.

The people of the city shook, as though someone had awoken them from a deep sleep. They saw Venor burning in the fire and began to open their eyes to reality.

Boris watched as they awoke to what had happened. "People of the city, you must know the truth about what has happened here," he said. They turned to him and listened as he spoke, telling the story of Venor and the King of Souls. Finally he swore to them his loyalty and honesty as their new leader, promising to lead them into a life of peace at last.

CHAPTER 18

Wolf Attack

It was almost dark by the time Aragel and Sivis had made it to the foothills of the Crystal Mountains. The jagged rocks and sharp crystals were a welcome sight compared to what they had experienced in Crystal City, but they made travelling in darkness dangerous. Deciding it was best to stop and wait for daylight, the two men found a little cave in the mountain wall and set out their sleeping mats for the night. They pulled out the few scraps of food that remained in their bags to silence their growling stomachs, while a pool of clear water nearby quenched their thirsty throats and filled their water pouches. Though the hill they had chosen to rest on was the lowest in the range, it still came them a good view of the winding path hey planned to follow the next day.

Night crept up behind them, and quickly the day turned to pitch black night. It grew colder, and the travellers huddled under the walls of the mountain for shelter. The wind blew past their ears, howling across the rocky slopes; every now and then small rocks would dislodge themselves from above and drop around them. Unable to sleep, Aragel woke and offered to keep watch for the next few hours while Sivis slept; when he woke, Aragel would take his turn to rest. So the two took turns to keep watch in the night, each one feeling sleepy the moment the other awoke. Silently they went on, until the sun shone its orange beams across the mountain tops at last.

* * *

Aragel was on watch when the night began to turn to day at last, and he saw the dark clouds looming above once again. The past few weeks had been so eventful that he had barely looked at the sky. Only when the first beam from the sun lit the clouds above them did he notice them again and remember the reason for his journey. He thought of the people at home and hoped fervently that they were well. He looked at Sivis, who was now stirring from his sleep, and inwardly prayed that he would be able to return safe to his mother.

"So where to now?" Sivis asked as he began to roll up his sleep mat and strap it to his pack.

"We'll have to head north down that path over there to Axter." Aragel looked up from the pool of water he had been drinking from and pointed towards a path that sloped down away from them. In the dim light of the early sun, he could not see past the bend in the road. "I hope it doesn't rain," he said looking at the sky.

"Ha ha. Very funny. All right, I'm done. Let's go then," said Sivis as he slung his pack on his shoulders.

The path Aragel had suggested crossed gentler terrain than those they had used before. Though the sharp rocks and crystals seemed daunting at first, both men learned quickly how to navigate a safe way through them and avoid getting hurt. Every now and then, they stopped to marvel at the natural phenomenon of these crystals, admiring their massive, clear structure and how they seemed to be so perfectly formed.

"Amazing, aren't they?" said Aragel, stopping to touch a particularly large crystal stalagmite. It felt cold, but not hostile.

"Yes, I wonder how they formed," said Sivis,

studying a cluster of small but sinister-looking pointed rocks.

"You think these mountains are magic?" Aragel asked.

"I don't know. It feels like they might be, and I remember my mum telling me when I was a little boy of the mystical things that happen in these mountains. She spoke of creatures that were half man, half bird, of forest nymphs and people who walked through these paths and never came back the same again. Mostly good things."

Aragel's ears pricked up at the mention of creatures that were half man and half bird. He remembered his dream back when he had still been travelling with Erien, and wondered how his friend was now.

"What did you use to do before all this madness started?" Sivis asked, breaking into Aragel's thoughts.

"Oh, nothing much; help my mum out on the farms, hang out with my buddies, Erien and Virto. I imagine you'd like them, they're good guys. Right now, they would be the ones helping me look after mother," Aragel said, panting a little as he talked. The path had now begun to slope upwards.

"Do you think you'll ever see them all again?"

"I don't know man, it's not something I really want to think about," said Aragel. "I wonder how Katharina's doing, too."

"Ah, the lovely Katharina." Sivis smiled.

"You never told me about your girlfriend," Aragel said.

"I told you what happened. What else do you want to know?"

"Well, what was she like and how did you meet her?"

"The usual, guy meets a girl in their village. It's a small village, Balwan, and everyone knows everyone. I saw Zuzana one day helping her father gather wood. Things were a lot different back then. Balwan was a quiet village. It was peaceful, and everyone was friendly and kind. Zuzana wasn't particularly pretty or anything, but she wasn't plain either. She had long dark hair and a rather flat nose. But there was something in her eye that caught me. Well, in her eye and her body," Sivis said cheekily. Aragel laughed. "She was well built and strong, and I suppose I'm just attracted to that sort of girl. You know, the outdoorsy type. She knew every hill and mountain that surrounded Balwan. She would explore places on her own and take me there afterwards. I learned things about Balwan and its people I had never bothered to think about before. That's why it came as such a blow when she died. I would have never expected her to slip and fall off the way she did. If one of us was clumsy, it was definitely me."

Aragel listened quietly to Sivis's story and thought about Katharina, wondering if he would ever get the chance to see what could have been. They continued chatting for a while about their lives and what they would have been doing if all the destruction had never happened.

The day passed uneventfully and soon the evening shadows were drawing in. The ground, they noticed, was softer now as they got further down the road and there were more trees on both sides of the path. Giant fir trees with stiff, greyish needles swayed in the icy wind. They were beginning to see snow on the path, and the travellers pulled on thick leather jackets for warmth.

It was not long before they began to notice pawprints on the ground. Aragel recognised them all too easily: wolves. There were only two options now, to eat or be eaten, and the travellers were starving. They had finished all their scraps the night before and needed a good meal. The wolves posed a threat, but perhaps this was also an opportunity.

A low growl came through the thick forestry on Aragel's left. He would not have heard it if his senses had not already been attuned to the sound. He turned to Sivis, who was walking cheerfully next to him. "There are wolves around us, I just heard one. We have to move quickly," he said. "Maybe this could even be a chance to get some fresh meat."

"Good plan! Meat for dinner tonight," Sivis said with an impish grin. After all this time, he still craved action; to get into the thick of a fight with a wild animal and taste the satisfaction of a well-earned kill. "Let's go," he said.

The two travellers separated quietly. The paths were obvious and there was little chance that they would lose each other as long as they stayed close to the trail. Aragel knew he was being watched from where he was, and he was getting nervous. He reached into his jacket to pull out his knife and brushed against the form-fitting armour on his chest, finding comfort in knowing that at least his torso was safe from harm.

Sivis walked stealthily on the opposite side of the track, like a predator on the hunt, his only goal now being to kill a wolf for food. Each made sure the other was always within sight. There was no further sound from the wolves as they walked, and they both wondered if maybe Aragel had heard wrongly; the footprints could be old ones.

Then suddenly Sivis felt a great blow as something heavy struck his shoulders – a full-grown adult white wolf. The animal's huge paws drove him to the ground and he collapsed with a yell and a loud thud, the wolf's teeth crushing his shoulder. With his hammer-wielding arm pinned down by the weight of the great beast, Sivis struggled desperately to wrestle free.

Hearing Sivis's yell, Aragel ran towards the sound, only to come face to face with another wolf, a black one, its eyes shining a deadly blue. Aragel stood, his dagger in one hand, as he and the wolf sized each other up. Aragel stared the animal in the eye, never taking his gaze off it. They circled one another and in a flash, the beast pounced on Aragel, throwing him to the ground; its teeth began to close on Aragel's exposed neck. Aragel thrust as hard as he could with his dagger, aiming for the heart, and with relief he felt the great beast turn limp. Then he struggled desperately to lift the great weight of the wolf from his body. At last he pushed it off and stabbed it once more in the neck to make sure it was truly dead.

"Ah, you got one too," Sivis said cheerfully, tossing his hammer up and down, grinning. Aragel got up, panting.

"You killed one?"

"Of course! With this little baby, it's hard to miss," he said kissing the hammer.

* * *

It was now nearing sunset in the Crystal Mountains

and the two travellers had found a dry ditch in which they could sleep for the night. They dragged their kills to the ditch and began preparing their dinner. Sivis, skilled with the knife, skinned the animals and disembowelled them, while Aragel prepared the fire for the night.

"The days are short and the nights are long here," said Sivis. "I'm thinking maybe we could stay a little while to plan our route and see if there's a shorter way. You have the map?"

Aragel nodded, his brow furrowing at the wood, which was refusing to burn. "But it's dangerous for us to stay here. There are so many wild animals around."

"No more than what's out there," Sivis pointed out. "It'd be safer for us to stay and plan our route well before we set off again. Besides, we've got food to last us a long while and we need to wait for the furs to dry before we can use them. I think we're better off here."

Aragel was not sure about this suggestion, but he did not argue. He did not have a better plan anyway.

They ate their fill for the night and sat beside the fire to keep warm. The sounds of the wild echoed all around them as they watched the embers of the fire glow red and orange. Tired from their long day, neither saw the need to speak, so they both stayed silent and indulged in their separate thoughts. Aragel thought about Erien, Katharina and everyone back in Arya, while Sivis dreamt of Mirya and silently asked Zuzana to keep watch over them as they walked through the mysterious Crystal Mountains. As the fire wore out, the two travellers slumped against the walls of the ditch, and dozed off quickly in the darkness.

CHAPTER 19

Zena

It was cold and miserable, just as it had been for the past few months; how long it had gone on like this, Erien had lost count. Packing his bags and preparing for his journey to see Aragel almost seemed like going on holiday away from this place. Cyrella had become more and more anxious, though she maintained her composure and never asked or spoke about Aragel. Erien had witnessed the lines on her forehead deepen over the past months since he had returned to Arya.

He had decided to move in with Cyrella to take care of her, since his brothers could take care of his parents.

He worried for Cyrella's health as he watched her walk out to the front gate of the house every evening after dinner to wait for her only son's return, her face full of hope that she would see her son healthy and safe walking down the slope leading towards their home. For every day that he did not return, the lines grew deeper, yet she never ceased to hope and continued her ritual of walking and waiting every evening.

The food they had stored in the soil beneath them had long been finished and they now depended on potatoes alone for survival; potatoes and the occasional wild creature that innocently wandered into their village. People were dying everywhere, disease was rampant and the cold pierced the hearts of everyone still alive. At least they still had some food, for which they would never fail to give thanks, despite their circumstances. That was the wonderful thing about the Aryans; they never failed to be grateful for what little they had despite their suffering.

"Come back inside, Aunt Cyrella," Erien gently coaxed her. "It's getting cold." She looked fragile standing outside on her own under the rising moon, her body thin and undernourished. Erien felt his muscles tense as he took her arm and escorted her back indoors. He was angry with Aragel for many reasons. He imagined that the first thing he would do when he saw him would be to swing a punch in his face and pummel him to the ground. Despite what everyone had said about how Aragel was smart, did not act rashly and did things for good reasons, it seemed highly irresponsible of him to have left Erien behind; Erien, who had nowhere left to go except back to Arya to deal with all of this; Erien, who was his best friend and had made it known that he would stick by Aragel through everything. He would not accept explanations about Aragel wanting to make this journey on his own, or feeling that it would be the safest option for him to go alone. To Erien, Aragel had been selfish, and that was all.

Yet, despite all the resentment he felt towards his selfish best friend, Erien still made up his mind to try to find Aragel. He did not know the way properly and was not sure if he would ever find him. He simply hoped that he would somehow find enough water and that the wild animals were now too weak to attack him.

***

Over in the city of Malur, Katharina and her family sat around the fireplace, sipping hot chocolate and chatting about their day.

"I wonder how Aragel is," Katharina mumbled, a faraway look in her eyes.

"I'm sure you do," her father quipped, his eyes twinkling.

"Oh stop it, father, you know nothing could have ever come out of that," said Katharina.

"As a matter of fact, I don't," he replied, grinning.

"Well there's no use in thinking about that, I was just saying that I hope he's safe," she said.

"I'm sure he is, he's a smart kid, he'll know how to take care of himself," Vaclar replied. "We've got to find a way to keep ourselves going. We've cleaned up the streets and done the best we could. We can't stop people from burning whatever they want to, everyone's cold. What'll we do for food when we run out? It feels like ages since I've tasted jam," he said, his thoughts drifting.

For weeks now, Malur had found itself in a state not far off from Arya. The only thing that seemed to grow now was wheat. There was nothing else, and whatever Katharina's family had left, they rationed carefully. The church was maintained as it had always been; almost as if that was the only way they could keep their hopes alive. Katharina often thought of Aragel and wondered if he was well and safe. She would find herself dreaming about him in her sleep and often wondered if she should go in search for him. She considered asking her father many times, but she knew he would never let her go. Her only chance would be to sneak out in the middle of the night. She knew the way to Axter, as she had heard her grandfather speak of it enough times for it to be ingrained in her mind. She knew the perils of travelling alone, much more of a woman travelling alone. But something lingered in her mind and had eaten away at her every day since Aragel had left. A part of her felt as though she was meant to go, yet another part knew the devastation her parents would feel if she left. She could not make them worry, not in a time like this.

Standing at the front gate of her house, Katharina looked up into the dark clouds, the cold wind biting her rosy cheeks as it blew through her hair. "Where are you, Aragel?" she whispered into the darkness. Lonely tears flowed from her eyes as she whispered a quiet prayer for the man whom she barely knew but felt she had known for lifetimes.

***

After crossing the last of the Crystal Mountain peaks, Aragel and Sivis came to a canyon. Looking down the steep drop, they saw a faint light shining from the mountainside. A steep and narrow pathway alongside the mountain led down to it.

"I think someone stays there," said Sivis, "and I think we should go down." He said dusting himself off.

He had put himself face down on the cliff's edge to get a clearer look of where the light might have been coming from.

"It might be dangerous though, we don't know who lives there, assuming there's anyone there in the first place."

"Won't know till we try," Sivis said, preparing to climb down. "Come on, we've got nothing to lose. Besides, we can't stay up here. Look around you, we're surrounded by spikes."

Aragel looked around and saw that indeed, tiny little black and blue spikes protruded from the ground. He had not noticed them before through the thick soles of his boots. They walked precariously down the winding and narrow path, bodies, arms and legs pressed up against the mountain wall as they grabbed at anything that could lend support. The narrow path widened as they drew nearer to the light and dead trees grew on the sides and rocks sat all around.

At last they came to a little house made of dark wood. The door was wide open and a single large candle burned in its holder on the window sill. The house appeared empty, prompting Aragel and Sivis to step inside.

"Empty house, shelter and warmth by candle light. Looks good to me man. Let's stay here," Sivis said, putting his backpack down on a table in the middle of what looked like a kitchen. There was a stove beneath the window sill and beside it, a small stack of firewood.

"What did you say?" came Aragel's muffled voice. He had wandered further into the house and saw that there was one other room apart from the one they had entered through. It looked like a bedroom, and a thin mattress lay with a blanket folded neatly upon it.

"I think we should stay here," Sivis repeated.

"Yes, I guess we could wait and see if the owner returns. Either way there's nothing to lose I suppose," Aragel said, putting his backpack on the table beside Sivis's.

The two walked around the little house, exploring it for any clues as to who might be living there, but found nothing. Eventually they decided to walk into the forest behind the hut, taking their belongings with them.

"I don't see why we couldn't have left our things there. There was no one there. It was abandoned," Sivis muttered, shifting his backpack higher up onto his back.

"And who lit the candle then? Don't be dumb, even if no one lives there, someone could still come along and take our stuff."

"But who?" Sivis retorted, annoyed that Aragel always seemed to have an air of knowing it all.

"Shh!!" Aragel suddenly hissed.

"That's a good comeback," Sivis said sarcastically.

"No! Look!" Aragel whispered, pointing at the ground in front of them. The form of a young woman lay motionless on the ground. Rocks were scattered around her, grey and dying trees towering over her lifeless body.

"Is she dead?" said Sivis.

"I don't know. Maybe we should leave her alone."

"But what if she isn't dead and she's just passed out and needs help?" said Sivis

"She's not injured," Aragel pointed out, looking at her more closely.

"You wouldn't know that," said Sivis. "She's lying in such an awkward position."

"I still think we should..." Aragel was about to say he thought they should leave her alone, but then a movement stopped him. The young lady stirred, rubbed her eyes, then opened them and sat up. When she saw Sivis and Aragel hovering over her, she let out a scream.

"Who are you?" she yelled, pushing herself backwards with her legs, her hand feeling about on the crystal-dusted ground as if she was looking for something. "Who are you and what do you want?" she screamed, even louder. Feeling her hand touch something hard on the ground, she grabbed at it and produced a bow. Before either man could reply, she had whipped out an arrow and put it in place, ready to shoot. "I'm an archer," she declared. "Come any closer and I'll kill you both with one arrow!"

"We're sorry," Aragel said, making the big mistake of taking a step towards the girl. Swoosh! An arrow darted from her bow and straight towards Aragel's torso. Aragel screamed as it grazed his side.

"What is the matter with you!" Sivis yelled at the lady.

"One step!" She yelled back, pulling out an arrow from her side. Sivis moved swiftly, kicking her off her feet and pinning her to the ground.

"Calm down!" he yelled.

"Let me go!" She screamed. "Let me go! No, no, no, no, not again! Please not again! Let me GO!" She wailed. Taken aback by her outburst, Sivis loosened his grip to show her that he was not going to hurt her, but held her down firmly enough to ensure she could not pull out another arrow.

"Calm down," Sivis said. "We're travellers, we come from the other side of the mountain and we are on our way to the Forest of Axter. We mean you no harm. We had found a house not far from here and waited there for any sign of people, but there were none, so we walked out here to see what else we could find and saw you sleeping. We thought maybe you were injured. And that's when you woke up."

Aragel let out a loud groan. Sivis looked over at him and saw that he was rubbing the spot where the arrow had grazed him. He had been quick enough to move and avoid a direct hit.

"Now if I let you go, will you calm down?" Sivis asked her. Frightened, the girl nodded. "Good," said Sivis as he slowly released his grip. She struggled a little and Sivis tightened his grip again. "I need to be able to trust you. I don't want to hurt you." Again, she nodded. "Now, what's your name?" Sivis asked, releasing her slowly.

"Why should I tell you? Who are you?" the girl replied.

"Still trying to be tough, eh? Look lady, if we wanted to hurt you, we would have done it by now. Fortunately for you, we're not interested in that. So, shall we call it a truce?"

The girl stayed silent, staring at Aragel and Sivis. Finally breaking the silence, she pointed at Aragel's wound. "You should get that looked at."

Aragel looked down to see blood oozing out of his side. "Damn it, yeah thanks. Know any doctors in the area?" he said without smiling.

"Well, fortunately for you, I used to be a midwife's assistant and I know a thing or two about wounds," she said, walking towards Aragel. "I'm sorry about that." she mumbled.

"Now what do I say to that?" Aragel replied casually.

"Well you two shouldn't have been standing over me like that!" she said. "I'm Zena, by the way."

"Zena," Sivis said, "interesting name. Where are you from?"

"Here. Well, I grew up in another town but it was taken over by the King of Souls and when the townspeople went crazy after everything had been taken from them, the men took their frustrations out on women."

"What do you mean? They hit you?" Aragel asked.

"They did more than that. They raped and killed as they pleased, thinking that would buy them more grace from the King of Souls if they presented the souls of the dead to him. The killing was because they feared him, the raping, was just for themselves." She looked away. Not knowing what to say, Sivis changed the subject.

"What were you doing lying on the ground like that?"

"Oh, that's something my father taught me when I was a little girl," she said, lightening up a little. "It's a trick. You lie on the ground and play dead. Soon animals draw near and sniff you. That's when you whip out the bow and arrow and get yourself some dinner," she said proudly. "By the way, that's my house you broke into."

Aragel and Sivis smiled in spite of themselves. It was hard not to like Zena; although she had an edge to her, she was endearing. Her past had clearly made her vulnerable, yet strong and independent.

"Was it always like this here? These mountains?" Sivis asked.

"Not at all. The crystals used to be so beautiful, clear and shiny. Always different shades of blue, never black. It was always peaceful, like I'd imagine heaven to be. The people of the Crystal Mountains always believed that this was heaven on Earth. But it all changed when the King of Souls made an appearance."

Aragel could not understand why the King of Souls seemed a bad person to Zena and the people of the Crystal Mountains. Had he not been kind to Katharina's family and looked after Malur? Had he not been forced to take souls to feed himself, and even then had only done so in humane ways? Why did it all seem so different here?

"He seemed like a good creature to most villages and towns, I've heard," Zena said as though reading Aragel's mind. "I don't know why it was so different here. I've only heard that he made a pact with the Raggotah when he was desperate and starved for souls that he would offer protection to certain parts in return for the souls they offered him."

Aragel listened quietly, trying to fit the pieces together. There were still many things he did not understand.

Zena turned out to be good company, and the two travellers wound up spending the next few days with her. She nursed Aragel's wound until it had recovered enough for them to go hunting, and they learned to hunt her way – to play dead and strike when animals came sniffing around you. For water, she surprised them by showing them a well that she had drilled herself and cleverly disguised with large rocks. She got along well with both Aragel and Sivis, but particularly with Sivis, who was attracted to her tough yet feminine ways.

"You can't have drilled this hole by yourself," Sivis commented when he saw the well for the first time.

"Well, you would have never thought you'd have a girl kick your butt either, until it happened," she retorted.

"Correction, not my butt, his butt," Sivis replied, gesturing towards Aragel. "I believed your butt got kicked by me." Zena laughed a little girl's laugh that made Sivis smile without realising it.

"You like me, don't you?" Zena, said holding his gaze.

Taken aback by her question, Sivis flushed and went back to chopping wood. "Well. What's not to like, right?" Sivis said smiling. He was attracted to her, but he knew they would not be staying long and he did not think it right to express how he felt towards someone he knew he would have to leave in a matter of days.

To display their gratitude, the two men offered to work for her, doing the tasks that Zena herself could not manage. They repaired the roof of the little house and dug her well deeper so they could draw more water. They spent almost a week together.

"I wish things were the way they were before," Zena muttered one day while they were out hunting. "We wouldn't be out here hunting for food. The real hunters would've been doing that."

"But then we wouldn't have met," Sivis replied with a smile. Zena caught his eye and looked away shyly. She liked him, but she knew he was a traveller and would have to leave soon. There was really no point in getting too fond of someone who was not going to be staying around.

After a few more days of hunting, cooking, laughing and exchanging stories together, Aragel finally spoke to his friend on his own.

"It's time to leave, Sivis," Aragel said one evening as they walked back from gathering wood.

"But we're getting on fine here. And Zena needs us. Who'll take care of her?" Sivis asked.

"That's exactly why we should leave, we can't get

too comfortable. I'm sure Zena will be fine without us. She'd done perfectly well without us up to now."

"But she's grown dependent on us. We can't leave her behind. What if she came with us?".

"No," came Aragel's firm reply. "It's too dangerous for her, Sivis, and she isn't the one who has grown dependent." He gave a knowing smile. "We've got to save our lands first before we think of anything else. That's why we're here, that's why your mother sent you here."

Sivis did not reply and looked away. Aragel was right and he knew it, but that did not mean he had to like the plan. He wanted to take Zena with him, but as Aragel said, it was too dangerous and they couldn't allow anything to happen to her.

CHAPTER 20

A Shocking Discovery

That night, they told Zena their plan to leave in the next two days. Zena looked at Sivis expectantly, but she knew in her heart that he would never allow her to venture out on such a dangerous mission. Over the past few days, Sivis had treated her like a princess and never allowed her to do anything alone. It was true that she had grown very fond of him and she could not quite bear to see him leave, but if everything they had told her so far was true, these two men seemed to be the only hope anyone had for things to get better.

So the two men set off, with Zena accompanying

them for the first part of the journey. Reluctantly she showed them the way through the Crystal Mountains and out onto the other side.

"She was great, wasn't she?" Sivis said. It had been two hours since Aragel and Sivis left Zena's house.

"Yeah, she was pretty nice," Aragel replied.

"I've never met a girl like her. Smart and feminine with an edge. I love how she fought for herself the first day we met, and what about that well she dug? She's a woman and she dug that well all by herself! I would have never been able to do that on my own." Sivis went on about Zena's many abilities while Aragel responded with the occasional 'mmms' and 'uh-huhs', trying to look interested.

For the next two days, Aragel and Sivis trudged across the crystalline wilderness towards the Forest of Axter. At first Sivis hoped that Zena would show up out of nowhere to rejoin them, but that never happened. Late on the third day they came to another house, and this time it was obviously empty. It was dark by the time they had reached the abandoned house, and it did not take them long to decide that they were going to sleep there for the night.

The little house was empty except for a few candles lying around. Sivis lit the candles while Aragel explored the house, looking for clues of occupancy, but found none. There were no mattresses on the floors of the single bedroom, no tables, and no chairs.

Outside the house, as the sun dipped lower, the silhouettes of giant twisted, curving trees seemed to loom larger in the twilight. Towering at twenty and thirty metres high, they looked from a distance like monsters contorted and frozen in strange positions. In the little candle-lit hut, the two men sat quietly on the hard wooden floor with their sleeping mats laid out beneath them, providing some warmth against the harsh cold. Their minds wandered, as they always did whenever they were silent. What was to happen next, neither of them knew.

***

Sivis broke the deafening silence. "Let's get going."

"Are you insane? No, we're staying here," Aragel replied.

"And wait for sleep? It's barely sundown. Come on man, there's no point in staying here staring into space. It's still early, and the moon's already rising. We could get some miles under our belts before dawn."

Sivis had a point. Sleep was not about to happen the minute he closed his eyes. Besides, it would keep Aragel's mind entertained and hopefully quieter. They blew out the candles in the hut before leaving, to erase any trace of their presence, and set off at last into the great Forest of Axter, heading for the strange twisted trees.

As they walked further into the gloom, Aragel hoisted his backpack higher up onto his shoulders. The weight of it was finally getting to him. Then suddenly, *thump, thump, thump!* A loud noise suddenly came from the darkness in front of them. The two men shot glances at one another, moving immediately into a back-to-back position, their eyes darting all around them. There was nothing in sight, but the sound echoing through the forest made their hair stand on end.

They moved forward, still with their backs to each other. Every few minutes, they would hear the strange thumping noise again. At times it seemed to be sounding from deep within the forest and at other times it seemed to be coming from the trees just two feet away from them. It was almost as if the trees had hollowed trunks and were creating the sounds within themselves.

The sound continued, but Aragel and Sivis eventually broke away from the trees and walked side by side until they reached an open grass patch and decided to settle down for the night. The entire night was filled with strange thumping noises coming from near and far, but the noises stopped as mysteriously as they had started at the first sign of daybreak.

"Time to go, Sivis." Aragel shook his slumbering friend.

"But it's still early," Sivis mumbled.

"Yes, but we've got to move as soon as the light comes up. It gets dark quickly here. Come on, let's go."

Aragel folded his sleeping mat up and they packed their bags and walked on, uncertain which direction to go in and hoping for clues to enlighten their journey. The trees of the forest amazed them as they walked on blindly. Tall, skinny tree trunks that were thin enough to wrap one's arms around fully stood so closely side by side that it felt as if they were trying to navigate their way out of a vast cage of trees. The silence lent them no clues; no sounds of rushing waters or animals or human activity. The only signs of life were the trees around them and the sound of their own breath.

"Anything in your grandfather's diary about whereabout in the Forest we're supposed to go?" Sivis asked.

"Nothing. He had only written about how to get here, nothing else," Aragel replied.

"Excellent. So what do we do now?" Sivis sighed.

"I don't know, just keep walking," said Aragel, shrugging and stepping on a long branch he had found along the way on the ground. The silence continued and the men eventually found a space large enough to start a fire and settle down again for the night.

"I think we should set up traps," said Aragel.

"What for?" Sivis asked. "We're not planning to stay here long, are we?"

"No, but what if animals come hunting in the middle of the night?"

"Animals? We haven't seen a single creature since the wolves. What makes you think there are animals around?" asked Sivis.

"The sounds last night," Aragel replied, looking around for sharp branches on the ground.

"Oh… right OK," said Sivis, remembering the eerie booming noises. "What do we need then?" He dropped his backpack. Sivis found some suitable branches and Aragel, with the use of his dagger and carving skills, fashioned a simple pitfall trap. Inside it stuck the wooden spears Aragel had whittled into the ground, sharp ends pointing upwards towards the sky. The trees around them bore wild berries and edible leaves, which the men had to make do as dinner for now. They built a fire for warmth and light beneath the thick canopy of the Forrest. Maybe in the morning there would be some kill for their meat-starved stomachs.

Thump thump thump… Aragel had no sooner nodded off than he woke again with a start. He looked around, but saw nothing. Sivis lay sound asleep next to him snoring steadily. *THUMP THUMP THUMP*. It sounded nearer than before. He had to find out where it was coming from. He sat upright and listened again, but there was no further sound. Deciding it was safer to stay put and allow Sivis to continue sleeping, Aragel pulled his coat tightly around him and went back to sleep.

* * *

The sound of rustling leaves awoke Aragel the next morning. For no reason, his heart seemed to be beating faster than usual. He gripped his chest and looked around for Sivis. His companion's sleeping mat and backpack were still there on the ground, but Sivis himself was nowhere in sight. Thinking maybe his friend had gone to hunt for food or explore their surroundings, Aragel decided he would wait with their belongings in case Sivis came back and found him missing.

The silence around him was total. Suddenly he craved the sound of rushing water, the sound of a human voice, animals rustling in the bushes, birds chirping, anything. He had left everything he loved to venture out into this forest and now, looking up at the dark clouds, he wondered if it was really worth it. It had been so many months since he first saw the clouds, so long that now they seemed normal to him. His journey seemed a part of his regular life now, so far away from the life he had once led. He had no idea where his adventure was going to lead him, and yet at this point he no longer felt like he cared. He did not even know if his family and everyone back home was alive.

He sat and tried to recall his journey from the beginning to pass the time, but by the time he got to the part where he had left Erien, he was tired and restless. He had now been waiting for Sivis for almost two hours, and he thought it could not possibly do much harm to walk a little way to look for him. Maybe something had gone wrong and he needed help.

He searched as far as he dared, given that he had left their belongings unattended, but Sivis was nowhere to be found. Aragel felt his heart beating faster again and sat down on the dry grass to calm himself. He could not shake off the feeling that something might have happened to Sivis, and he could not bear the thought of his companion coming to harm. Finding his way back to their resting place, Aragel gathered bits of dry wood from around him and built a fire. If Sivis had got lost, the smoke would send out a signal of sorts to help him to find his way back.

During the evening he managed to trap a rabbit and prepared it for his meal. Darkness came earlier than the night before, and Aragel was glad he had gathered enough firewood to last through the night. He sat staring at the rabbit cooking on the fire and wondered why Sivis would have left without saying anything. He thought back to Sivis's mother, wondering if she might have mentioned anything that could provide a clue as to why Sivis would have left so suddenly. It seemed such a long time since he had left Erien, and it all seemed so far away now. He wondered if Erien hated him for leaving him behind.

He ate the rabbit slowly, cleaning off each bone as though he would not see meat again for a while and wondering if Sivis had had anything to eat for the night. He considered for a while if maybe Sivis's disappearance was the work of someone trying to take revenge, but he could not figure out why anyone would want to do that.

Aragel hardly slept that night, ironically since there was no thumping or any other noise to distract him. He would have chosen the thumping noise over Sivis's absence any time.

The next morning the sky was a misty, dirty grey and the Forest was darker than usual as Aragel to set off once again to look for his friend. As he walked, he stared closely at the mist in front of him, squinting to focus on the tiny mist particles, which almost seemed like black soot. Combined with the dark sky, they cast a grey, flat light over everything. A sense of déjà vu consumed him as memories of his father and the stories he often told of the Forest flooded his mind, pulling his attention away from the gloom around him. He immersed himself in his thoughts, barely taking notice of the way he was going and simply following his instincts.

Suddenly he stopped. Just ten metres away from him a man lay slumped against a tree. It was Sivis.

"Sivis!" Aragel called out. He ran towards his friend, calling again, but there was no response. Sivis simply lay there, his eyes staring into space. "No, no, no, no, Sivis!" Aragel screamed at him. He knelt down next to his friend and tried to shake him by the shoulders, but something was very odd; his hands went through him as if he wasn't there. He tried again, but although his unconscious friend looked solid enough, it was like to trying to take hold of a cloud.

Suddenly Sivis's head spun round to face Aragel, while his body stayed still. Startled, Aragel stumbled backwards. He stared into Sivis's lifeless eyes and saw no expression, no sign of life.

Unable to believe what he was seeing, Aragel went into a frenzy. "Sivis, Sivis talk to me, man! Come on, wake up! What are you playing at? It's not funny man, wake up!" Aragel rambled on as he waved his hands in front of Sivis.

Aragel sat back, despairing, with no idea what to

do next. Suddenly Sivis's hand moved, and his limp fingers picked up a stick from the leaves around him and seemed to be trying to signal with it. But then the hand stopped midway.

Maybe Sivis was under some sort of spell, which meant it ought to wear off. Aragel decided to build a fire and stay with him till daybreak, so he left his friend there by the tree and went off to gather wood. He took an old shirt from his pack and wrapped it around a thick branch to form a torch. He lit it, and with rage and sadness filling his heart, held it close to Sivis's body. In the glow of the torch, he saw that it seemed a little cloudy now; it no longer looked as well-defined as a body and seemed almost smudged, as if someone had put a cloud over it. As if it was fading away...

Sorrow coursed through Aragel's entire body, and he fell to his knees and wept. He cried out to the silence, but all he heard in return was his own echo bouncing off the trees. He stared into the darkness, his heart filled with despair.

It was a while before he noticed a flicker of orange light in the distance. "Sivis, look," he said, still unable to believe his friend was not going to come back to life at any moment. There was no response. "Sivis, there's a light there, we have to go and check it out. Listen, I'm going to take a look. You stay right where you are and I'll come back for you, OK?" No response.

He got up and walked towards the light. As he drew closer, he saw that it was a fire, and around it were sitting a row of dark figures, all facing the flames. He counted them; there were ten. One of them looked up when he saw Aragel approach them.

"Er - hello," Aragel began. There was no reply. The figures regarded him silently. They did not look threatening, but still they said nothing.

Aragel went on to tell them who he was and what he was doing in the Forest. "I have a friend and he's hurt," he said. "There's something wrong with him. I don't know if it's some sort of a spell or if he's sick. But he's alive. I know he's alive. He moves, he just doesn't respond to sound..." Aragel trailed off. "You have to come and help me."

"He's dead, boy," came a voice from one of the dark figures.

"No, no, he's not. Didn't you hear what I said? I said he moved, he was able to move on his own," Aragel argued.

"That's because his soul is still there," said another of the figures. He looked up, allowing the light from the fire to illuminate his features. He looked old, with greying hair and dark, sunken eyes.

"He's dead, son. That's how they all die here in the Forest. Their souls hang around for a while because they're not sure where to go. But the more you hang around them, the harder it is for the soul to depart. So you've got to leave your friend and let him find his own peace."

"I can't leave him!" Aragel exclaimed. "What will I tell his mother? I promised her his safety!"

"It probably wasn't your fault," said the elderly man. "Things happen in the Forest that no one can explain. If his mother allowed him to come here, she probably knew the dangers. The Forest takes as it gives." Aragel did not understand this cryptic comment.

"I need to find the Forest Nymphs. Do you know where they are?" Aragel asked suddenly, feeling as though only they could help him now. The figures grew silent. "Where are the Nymphs?" Aragel asked again. The same man looked up at Aragel and pointed toward the west.

"Look beyond the hill of rocks and search below the roof of trees," he said, speaking in a poetic rhythm. Wasting no time, Aragel took to his feet and ran.

It did not take him very long to reach a hill of rocks, which was shaded over with a roof of tree canopies. A faint white light shone from it, and Aragel felt his heart lighten a little. Somehow he felt there was still hope. The most important thing at the moment was saving Sivis if possible, but his best hope of doing that was to find the Nymphs.

In the distance through the trees he could now see the source of the light. Strangely it seemed to be coming from a row of glowing human figures. He walked over the hill of rocks until he was on its far side. The white figures were now clear, and he could see that just like the dark figures, they were seated in a motionless circle.

But as Aragel drew nearer he felt all his hopes disappear in a flash. If these were indeed the Forest Nymphs, they appeared to be lifeless. They sat as still and cold as stone. The faint white glow he had seen was emanating from their pale, bloodless skin, and they were staring into space with dead, cold eyes.

Aragel felt a terrible sense of sadness. Surely now there was no more hope left. If the Nymphs were gone, that meant his entire journey had been for nothing. All the towns, the cities of filth and gore, his ordeal in prison, leaving his friends and family behind. It had all been for nothing.

The weight of his despair slowed him down as he walked back to the place where the dark figures were sitting. Aragel did not know who they were or where they were from, but at least they were alive.

The fire had dwindled now. He looked around at each one and finally mustered the energy to ask, "Who are you? Where are you from?"

One by one they looked up, their faces becoming

visible beneath their dark hoods as the light shone on them. They looked at Aragel and without a word turned back to face the fire. Aragel understood now that they had all faced the same thing. Each of these men had come in search of the Forest Nymphs, only to find them frozen in death.

Tired and broken, Aragel walked quietly forward and found a space between two of the figures. Then he sat down, the eleventh shadow.

Aragel stared into the fire. What was to become of him and all he cared about?

THE END

COMING SOON:
Forest Nymphs: Into the World of Shadows